He turned his head and she got a shock; he was less than twenty, with dark brown eyes, beautifully tanned skin, and hair, that with the light behind it, haloed into a blond aureole. She felt a floating sensation; her knees went weak and her breath got short. In her own mind, her own voice said quite clearly, "You're the most beautiful thing I've ever seen," and for one awful moment she wasn't sure that she hadn't said it aloud.

"Hi," said the stranger. His voice was low and soft . . . secret. A wave of feeling passed through Jenny, who felt she had to find a place to sit immediately.

Dear Readers:

Thank you for your many enthusiastic and helpful letters. In the months ahead we will be responding to your suggestions. Just as you have requested, we will be giving you more First Loves from the boy's point of view; and for you younger teens, younger characters. We will be featuring more contemporary, stronger heroines, and will be publishing, again in response to your wishes, more stories with bittersweet endings. Since most of you wanted to know more about our authors, from now on we will be including a short author's biography in the front of every First Love.

For our Book Club members we are publishing a monthly newsletter to keep you abreast of First Love plans and to share inside information about our authors and titles. These are just a few of the exciting ideas that First Love from Silhouette has in store for you.

Nancy Jackson
Senior Editor
Silhouette Books

LAND'S END
Becky Stuart

First Love from Silhouette

Published by Silhouette Books New York

America's Publisher of Contemporary Romance

First Love from Silhouette by Becky Stuart

SILHOUETTE BOOKS, a Division of Simon & Schuster, Inc.
1230 Avenue of the Americas, New York, N.Y. 10020

Copyright © 1984 by Stuart Buchan

Distributed by Pocket Books

ISBN: 0-671-53397-5

First Silhouette Books printing June, 1984

10 9 8 7 6 5 4 3 2 1

America's Publisher of Contemporary Romance

Printed in the U.S.A.

For Schwarz and Fox

*We know not who we are
nor who we yet shall be. . . .*

JENNY

Prologue

Cassie," Jenny said. Cassie didn't hear her.

At the sound of Jenny walking across the room, he turned, just his head, and she got a shock: she saw he was less than twenty, with dark brown eyes, fair, beautifully tanned skin and hair that, with the light behind it, haloed in a blond aureole about his head. At the sight of her he smiled and his lips parted to show white, even teeth, and as the grin spread across his face, Jenny felt a sensation passing through her that was quite unlike anything she had ever felt before: her knees went weak and her breath got short and she found that she had started to smile herself as though somehow his smile was coaxing a smile back from her.

In her mind, her own voice said quite clearly, "You are the most beautiful thing I've ever seen," and for one awful moment she wasn't sure that she hadn't spoken the words aloud.

Cassie said, "Oh, this is Jenny, my granddaughter."

"Hi," said the stranger softly. Spreading one big hand and slowly fanning it in a gesture of greeting at Jenny. His voice was low and soft . . . secret. Another wave of this new feeling passed through Jenny, who felt as though she really had to find some place to sit down.

1

Hi." His fair hair had been bleached by the early spring sun, his skin tanned a golden peach, and the smile hit her like a blow. "I'm Thorn," he said tilting his head slightly. "Remember me?"

Of course she remembered him. He was the new gardener Cassie had hired during spring vacation.

He reached out to help her down from the train. She saw that his hands were rough from gardening work and that his forearm where his shirt was turned back flexed with the muscle of someone who had been doing some heavy digging.

"I remember you," Jenny said, coaxing a smile from her face. Her whole body seemed to have gone weak at the sight of him. He was bigger than she remembered him. She had thought of him during the last term at school, half expecting to be called to the headmistress's office to be told that Cassie had been murdered by the new gardener. Once in a while his face had floated unbidden into her mind as she daydreamed, looking out the window of a classroom at the new grass of spring, the budding of the apple trees and the quick darting flights of the birds as they reveled in the new warmth, but slowly she had forgotten the details. The way that his nose snubbed slightly, that his eyes were almost gold, that his cheekbones when he turned away, as he did now to lift her luggage off the train, caught the sunlight and gave his face an almost Indian look, mysterious and powerful.

"Cassie sent me," he said, throwing another of his smiles at her. His teeth were small and even and very white in the tanned face. "She said not to be mad at her for not coming herself but she wanted to be home at Land's End when you got there." He lifted both suitcases that contained half as many books as clothes and weighed as much as Jenny herself. "We've really worked on the old place."

Jenny followed his swinging stride across the parking lot to Cassie's old yellow Buick convertible. The faded checked shirt stretched across his broad back as he lifted the two suitcases effortlessly into the back of the car. He opened the door for her and she slid in. Then he walked slowly around the front of the car as though there was all the time in the world, before he slid into the seat beside her.

Jenny thought she had seldom seen a young man who was so self-possessed. She wondered what his background was and asked suddenly, "How old are you?"

His reply was to laugh at her, a deep chuckle that seemed as much full of surprise as the joy of living. "What difference does it make?" he asked.

"None," she admitted, and waited for him to answer her anyway, but instead he started to hum as he spun the wheel on the old car and turned off the main street to the dirt road that led to the shore.

It took a few seconds for Jenny to recognize the tune, and when she did, she had an unpleasant rolling feeling in her stomach as though someone had broken into the house. He was humming Cassie's favorite tune—a tune Cassie only hummed when she was extraordinarily happy, a tune that Cassie claimed had been the first music she had ever danced to with Jenny's grandfather.

But before Jenny could speak, Thorn turned to face her again, and without a word, one thick lashed eyelid closed in a wink that brought the blood rushing to Jenny's face. He kept staring at her as she tried to cover her embarrassment and his lips twitched in a smile before he turned back to his driving.

Jenny lay her head on the worn headrest and closed her eyes, enjoying the sweet smell of the chestnut trees, imagining in her mind's eye the old, familiar road down which they were driving. She had driven this road every summer of her life from the time when she was a very little child and her parents were still alive. In those days they had come in a station wagon and Jenny would press her nose against the window of the back seat, her old spaniel, Max, hugged tight beside her. Max would be as excited as Jenny as he recognized the road and memories of sand dunes and chasing seagulls rose out of the ragbag of his old mind.

With her eyes closed, Jenny could remember how Max had smelled. No matter how often he was bathed he always had a doggie smell that made grownups push him away, but Jenny had loved it.

Land's End. Jenny opened her eyes. She knew by instinct that the house was nearby. Right on schedule she saw the top chimneys of the mansion above the pale-leaved chestnut trees. She knew that this year the house had to go, even if it was sold to the summer people who wanted to tear it down and build a dozen little summer houses along the beach, because there was no money any more even to keep up the basics. The long row of willows by the stream passed on the right and then, as familiar as the long-remembered smell of old Max, there was the oak tree where the driveway began. Then they were through the stone gateposts in one swift movement of the steering wheel by Thorn and passing beneath the cool shade of the poplar trees that stood as sentinels along the drive-way.

Thorn swung the wheel again and the car passed out of the shadow of the drive. The sunlight blinded Jenny. When she opened her eyes, the car had passed around the tall fountain set in the middle of the drive. She cried out for there was Land's End, her dear, familiar old falling-down house.

But today the whole vast front shone with a new white paint job and the shutters were bright green and the vines that had grown upchecked, like a birthmark over the west wing had been cut back so that they had flowered again in a pale yellow wisteria bloom.

Involuntarily she looked at Thorn who had slowed the car to a stop in front of the door. He was smiling at her in an open happiness. "You approve?" he asked.

"But who painted it?" Jenny asked, looking at the whole long front of the house.

"I did," he said.

"But we used to have a painter who did nothing but paint the house inside and out all year," Jenny said.

Thorn shrugged but the smile didn't go. "I just did the outside," he said in mock sorrow. "Didn't take as long."

Jenny wanted to reach out and hug him and might have, if at that very moment the front door hadn't been flung open on its hinges and Cassie hadn't erupted out of the house waving her arms.

15

"Welcome home, darling," Cassie said, pulling Jenny into her arms. Jenny hugged her tiny grandmother, feeling the happiness as Cassie held onto her tightly, and Jenny voluntarily looked up over her grandmother's shoulder at the gleaming front of the house.

2

Inside the house was unchanged. The wallpaper in the hall was stained from years of dampness and the staircase that led up to the second floor still missed a support. The silence inside was the same as it had always been, a soft quiet that fell over them as they walked across the black and white marble floor. It was the loveliest quiet Jenny had ever known, one she thought about in the long dark nights at school when she lay awake in the dormitory and listened to the breathing of the other girls—the sounds they made talking in their sleep, their grunts and moans and sounds without meaning.

She drew a deep breath, feeling safe as she always had at Land's End. She smiled over Cassie's head at the tall, fair boy who stood so near, towering over tiny Cassie. She could hear his breathing in the soft

17

silence of the house as the light fell now on his face, making his eyes shine brightly as he watched her. Slowly the smile started, the sides of his lips turning up tentatively, and the light in his eyes brightened. Jenny had one moment in which she wondered if it was a trick, something he had learned to do with that marvelous face, but then the smile hit her again with its full force, and she was smiling too.

That smile was like a gift, she thought, as across Cassie's head he whispered, "Welcome home, Jenny."

Jenny shivered, a long shaking of her body that passed from her shoulders all the way down to her toes.

The moment broke. Cassie stood back and said to her loudly, "Darling, you're cold! It's that awful train; let me heat you some soup." She dropped her arm from about Thorn, and taking Jenny by the hand, gently pulled her toward the kitchen.

Jenny followed; by the door into the hallway that led to the kitchen she turned to look again at Thorn who, a minute ago, had been standing there with her suitcases, but he had vanished, and her suitcases too.

Cindy and Jenny were riding on the train back to school last spring, when Thorn had already begun to occupy a place in her mind. Outside the window, the slums of New York had given way to the neat, manicured lawns of the suburbs. Cindy, plump and healthy as ever from two weeks with her father in California where she was allowed to eat anything and everything she wanted, was busy making a list in a red leather bond notebook on the cover of which she had written in large letters: THE DEFINITIVE CENSUS OF THE WORLD.

"Strange," Jenny said.

Cindy looked up from her notebook. "Well, everybody's strange," she said. "All the interesting people, anyway," she added.

Cindy was Jenny's best friend and had been for as long as either of them could remember. They had gone to nursery school together in New York back when Jenny's parents were still alive, and then later when Jenny had gone to live at Land's End with Cassie for grade school, Cindy had come out to stay for a few weeks every summer. Cindy loved Land's End almost as much as Cassie, and if she had had her choice, she would have lived out there permanently. As it was, Cindy was shuttled back and forth between her two warring divorced parents. Half the time she was with her father in California and was allowed to have anything she wanted to eat, and the other half she trailed after her restless mother, Daisy, who had gone through two more husbands since Cindy's father. Daisy was obsessed with staying young and thin, and when Cindy was with Daisy, she was kept on whatever diet Daisy was currently on.

He's . . . secretive, Jenny thought.

"Alesanadro di Scioipe," Cindy said, scribbling in her notebook, "number four hundred and twenty-two."

"There had to be only two thousand people in the world." Cindy was reasoning aloud as she scribbled in her notebook. "Everywhere I went, I met the same people. I mean there I was in California and *I hadn't met one person I didn't already know.*"

There was a clear and simple reason for that. Cindy's father was a very successful motion picture producer and her mother was one of the richest divorcées in America, so Cindy lived in a world of very rich people. Very rich people all hung out at the same places.

But Jenny knew there wasn't any sense in telling Cindy something as simple as that. Cindy, like Cassie, had a way of going deaf when she didn't want to hear something.

"So I marched right out and bought a notebook and started right in listing everyone I knew. If a law was passed and everyone was forced to do the same thing and we could run all the lists through a computer, I'm sure we'd find that there are only two thousand people in the world, and it's all a plot to make us think there is a population explosion."

Greenwich slipped away behind the train and Jenny settled into the soft rhythm of the wheels, like the waves that broke hour after hour, year after year on the beach in front of Land's End.

Cindy had a new theory. Cindy had almost as many theories as Daisy had diets. Cindy's new theory was that the population explosion was all a propaganda myth.

"I tell you, girl," Cindy was saying, "this theory of

mine is going to revolutionize world thought. I was sitting there in the Polo Lounge in Beverly Hills with Dad and suddenly it came to me as clear as a telegram: there are only two thousand people in the world."

Sometimes Jenny wondered if Cindy believed some of her own outrageous statements. She was sure she couldn't. Yet there were ways in which Cassie and Cindy were much alike. They both lived in their own worlds.

At the thought of her grandmother, Jenny's own mind wandered back to the house by the shore. Land's End would surely have to be sold this year. The old house had been for sale five summers now, ever since Cassie had realized that the trust was running out. But though everyone wanted to live in the Hamptons, no one wanted to take on a house the size of Land's End. The only offers had been from real estate people who wanted to buy the house for the land and tear it down to build a lot of little summer houses crowded side by side along the edge of the water. Last year's handyman had staked the dunes with a winding fence of narrow stakes and wire to hold the sand back, but the wind and sea were eating away at the land again. Already the old boathouse with the Chinese pagoda roof was settling into the water at the mouth of the marsh where the river ran into the sea. Soon all of Land's End would look like the boathouse, faded, falling down.

This year Cassie would have to agree to let the developers buy the land. "And what's more," Cindy was saying as Jenny came back to the present, "half the people I know look exactly alike, so when I've finished giving everybody a number, I'm going to start in on a second theory that in a hundred years we're all going to look alike; there will be one model for women and one model for men and that will be it."

Jenny could have answered that one too: the reason that half the people Cindy knew looked exactly like the other half is that they all bought their clothes at the same places and had their hair done by the same stylists. But she kept quiet about that, too, because an image of a tanned fair face had come to her mind, a face with pale green eyes and blond hair that fell over an unlined forehead, giving secret shadows to eyes with their own secret smile.

Another of Cassie's waifs. Last year it had been a painter who wanted to use the apartment over the old carriage house as a studio, and the year before, it had been a half-crazed professor who tried to live on seaweed that he gathered himself each day on the beach until he collapsed of malnutrition in mid-July and had to be hauled off to Southampton Hospital in a coma on the back seat of the Buick. Every year Cassie found one, some stray who was willing to help around the house and garden for nothing in return but room and board.

But none of them had been like Thorn. Thorn was tall and strong and could have gotten a good job at the beach club as a lifeguard or at any of the expensive restaurants as a waiter. Waiters made a lot of money in the summer. Last summer Randy Oakes had made eight thousand dollars and bought himself a new motorcycle. Jenny knew that for a fact because two weeks after he bought it, he skidded coming off the Montauk highway and spent all of September in the same hospital room that the professor had used the summer before.

Why would a boy like Thorn want to spend the summer working around Land's End?

The early spring twilight fell across the landscape. Cindy was quiet, listing name after name in her red notebook, as the world outside the train was lost to the night and the lights came on in the carriage. The regular rhythm of the wheels soothed Jenny into a sleep where she was back at Land's End and the waves were pounding on the beach and Cassie was calling her from across the dark lawn. In her dream Jenny woke, ran down the old stairs and across the black and white marble hall toward the water and Cassie's voice. But when she reached the top of the dunes the moonlit beach was quiet, but for the sea scalloping in softly across golden sand. A tall, blond boy stood with his arm about Cassie, and Cassie, seeing Jenny, said, "Darling, this is Thorn. He's to be our gardener this summer." Jenny woke to find Cindy staring at her.

"I was dreaming," she said.

"Spare me such dreams," Cindy said. "You were calling out this strange sound."

"What?"

"Mourn, mourn," Cindy said. "Are you okay?"

The other people in the carriage had been watching. Now they settled back into their own concerns. Other girls going up to school giggled and went back to their own gossip.

The landscape outside was a black mat, now pierced with the tiny lights of far-off Vermont farmhouses.

"Thorn . . ." Jenny said. Her heart had calmed down.

"Whatever," Cindy said, packing away her red notebook into an expensive leather valise. "You sounded like you were drowning or something."

"He's the new gardener," Jenny said.

Cindy was peering into the darkness, looking for some sign of where they were. "So?" she asked, lost in her own thoughts of the tortures ahead for her at school. Cindy was overweight and self-absorbed and every school term was misery from beginning to end.

"So we don't have any money to pay a gardener," Jenny said, returning to her earlier thought of why a strapping, young man like Thorn would want to spend a summer working around Land's End. "Not real money, that is."

Cindy looked at Jenny. *"Not* a very smart gardener," she said, and any further discussion of Thorn was lost at the sight of the conductor, throwing open the door at the end of the carriage. "Woods' Head," he cried. "Woods' Head."

The other girls going up to school leapt to their feet and started to pull down their satchels. Jenny and Cindy took theirs off the top rack as the lights of the small village came into view.

The train slowed and Cindy and Jenny waited with the other girls until the steps were let down. They got off into the cold Vermont spring night with the stars bright overhead and Miss Zack, the sports director, waiting for them by the old green school bus.

"Welcome, girls! Welcome, girls!" she cried at the sight of the returning students.

Jenny followed the other girls onto the bus. Thoughts of Thorn and why he was at Land's End drifted away, pushed out of her mind by Miss Zack's relentless goodwill and speculations as to what the last term at school would be like.

3

Cassie said, "Thorn borrowed a rotor tiller and turned the soil on the back pasture. The back pasture hasn't been seen since your father was a child." The happiness in her voice as she looked out over the half acre of field was contagious.

"But who will look after all this?" Jenny asked.

"We will," Cassie said with excitement. "Thorn has a plan."

Jenny looked down the row of neat furrows to where Thorn was dragging the perforated garden hose they'd bought that morning in town.

Jenny had lain awake much of the night after Thorn had woken her coming in at three o'clock. Where could he have been, she wondered, and after that, who was he? She had tried to think of a casual way to ask him, but nothing came to mind, and finally she had dropped off to sleep.

When she awoke, sunlight fell in a gold patch inside her window, and she stretched lazily, savoring the joy of not being woken by a school bell and not having to get up. The whole glorious summer stretched ahead.

When she got up, showered and dressed, she was lured downstairs by the smell of bacon and hot coffee. Cassie was in the kitchen, bent over a brown paper bag with a pencil. For all her disorder, Cassie still had one economy left over from her own father's time. She could never use a clean sheet of paper to make a list. Instead she cut open supermarket bags and made long lists of schemes on them.

"There you are!" she said, leaping to her feet when Jenny came into the kitchen. "The bacon's in the warming oven. How do you want your eggs?"

Jenny poured herself a cup of coffee from the blue enamel pot on the big range. "Scrambled." She sat on a stool near where Cassie had been sitting. "This is the best day of the year," she said.

Cassie was whipping the eggs. "Why?" she asked, smiling broadly.

"Oh, I don't know," Jenny said, thinking. "Maybe because school is over for another year. Everything's perfect on the first day of summer."

Cassie laughed. "I always thought of the first day of summer as the day they took down the shutters on the vegetable stands along the highway."

Jenny had turned over Cassie's brown paper bag. "What's this?" she asked.

"Oh, that. That's the garden," Cassie said.

Jenny looked at the rough plan. Something seemed wrong. "How big is it?" she asked finally.

Cassie was turning the skillet to let the butter melt evenly. "An acre," she said.

Jenny choked, spitting coffee across the counter. "An acre!" she exclaimed.

Cassie dropped the skillet and pounded Jenny on the back until she got her breath back.

"An acre!" Jenny repeated. "Who are you planning to feed? The whole summer population?"

"No, just part of it," Cassie said. She went back to the stove, dropped in the hot mixture of eggs and started to stir them. "Thorn thinks we can sell the vegetables to the stands along the highway and make enough money to fix the house," she said musingly. For a second her good spirits seemed to sag. She turned with the spatula raised. "Jenny, we simply *have* to sell Land's End this year, darling. If we don't . . ."

Jenny had been about to exclaim that she thought Thorn was taking a lot of authority around here, what with digging up land and deciding what they would do with it and how the money was to be spent, but now at the sight of the worry in her grandmother's eyes, some of her own concerns of the night before came back. She took a deep breath and said, "Don't worry, Cassie. We will. And even if no one wants the house as it is, someone will want it for the land."

"Yes," Cassie said worriedly, "but I'm afraid it's worse than that—the trust is running out."

Cassie had a small trust which Jenny and she had lived on. There had always been just enough money to keep up the tax payments on the house and pay for their living.

Jenny closed her eyes slightly, looking out the kitchen window at the hawthorn hedges. Adults had so many problems. Sometimes she wanted to grow up fast, and other times, she just wanted to climb up the stairs to the old nursery and crawl into bed. She could remember rainy, stormy nights when she was curled under the covers with an old cloth bear and the shutters were groaning in the wind and rain whipping in off the ocean. She would lie there knowing that Cassie was downstairs. When you were a child, other people took care of you, but when you grew up . . .

She didn't finish that thought, for the tall tanned figure of Thorn with his shirt off, came around the corner of the hawthorn hedge dragging a mower. She watched the play of sunlight on the muscles of his back as he pulled the old hand mower across the lawn toward the front of the house.

"Where did Thorn come from?" she asked abruptly.

Cassie looked up. "You were here when he first came," she reminded Jenny.

"No, I mean where did he really come from?" Jenny said. "Where did he grow up?"

Cassie was sliding the scrambled eggs onto a plate. "The South, somewhere," she said. "He doesn't talk about his childhood." She began cutting up a tomato. "Our tomatoes will be much better than this," she said, letting the questions drift away the way she so often did. Cassie was curious to a fault about some things, but she had her own rules about privacy. "Thorn thinks that we'll be able to make a nice profit selling the produce. That will help us get by for the summer."

But Jenny wasn't to be put off that easily. "Didn't you ask him?"

Cassie placed the slices of bright red tomato along the edge of a plate. "My father always said," she said, and Jenny could have repeated word for word what she was about to hear, "that you shouldn't ask personal questions. If a person wants you to know, they'll tell you."

Jenny had a brief picture of Cindy right then— Cindy who was relentless in her questioning—but she didn't pursue it. She knew that if she asked any more questions, Cassie would get her own stubborn look, the one where she would quietly block the answer to anything that she disagreed with and then slowly lead into a lecture on manners and deportment. For all her seemingly wild and bohemian outlook, Cassie had been a stern disciplinarian when she had raised Jenny, and Jenny was grateful for it. But most of Cassie's rules were old-fashioned, ones that she had learned from her own father, Jenny's great-grandfather, whom Cassie had worshipped.

When she was sure that Jenny had dropped the subject of Thorn's childhood, Cassie brightened and brought the breakfast plate over to Jenny by the window. Cassie went back to the stove and scrubbed it with a damp cloth while Jenny thoughtfully ate her breakfast staring out the window. Thorn came back twice, once taking a tool to edge the lawn, and the second time wiping sweat from his brow.

"He works hard," she said grudgingly.

"Yes, I think he's had a hard life, dear," Cassie said gently, which was as far as Cassie would go.

Jenny took her plate to the sink and ran hot water. She soaped the plate and rinsed it before putting it in the rack. "And a dishwasher," she said aloud.

"What?" Cassie asked. She was making another list.

"Oh." Jenny laughed. "I wasn't really saying anything. I was just thinking that if I had my own apartment, I would have all the modern conveniences like air conditioning, doormen and dishwashers."

Jenny realized instantly that she had hurt Cassie without meaning to. Cassie didn't say anything, but the small smile that had played at the corners of Cassie's mouth vanished.

"Oh, Cassie!" Jenny said. "I didn't mean that."

Cassie shook herself, throwing off her gloom. "No, you're right," she said. "I'm just too sentimental about this old house." She looked around the kitchen. "I'm not blind, you know," she said without rancor. "But when you love somebody or some place, you don't see all the faults that other people do. Sometimes I come into this room, or I'm walking through the hall and I see the wear and tear and . . . well, I'm made embarrassed." She sighed. "But Jenny, you should have seen the place when I was young. Land's End was the most beautiful house there ever was."

Jenny went over to Cassie and put her arm about her. "I've always loved Land's End, Grandmother," she said, using the word *grandmother* in one of her rare instances.

Cassie looked up at her. "But it's the past, isn't it?" Cassie said.

"Yes," Jenny admitted. "But," she added brightly, "we have one last summer and we can make it the best."

"And we have Thorn," Cassie said, hearing the sound of tools being dropped on the flagstone terrace outside the kitchen.

Some of Jenny's false brightness dimmed at that, but before she took the time to make Cassie give at least some thought to the strangeness of having a boy they knew nothing about living in the house, the door opened and there he was. Jenny wondered how long he had been out there, and if he had opened the door because he had knocked over the tools. But she put that thought away quickly as unworthy and suspicious.

Thorn had thrown on an old torn T-shirt that was

damp where it touched his body and his hair was slicked back from his forehead. The kitchen was one of the biggest that Jenny had ever seen, but Thorn managed to make the room seem small. She felt she couldn't breathe, as though there was not enough air for all of them, now that he had come into the room. She dropped her arm from around Cassie and said, "Okay, General. What chores today?"

Thorn had stopped a few feet inside the door. He looked inquiringly from Cassie to Jenny to see if Jenny was joking or being sarcastic. Jenny snapped a quick salute. "Reporting for duty," she said.

Cassie laughed. "Oh, what fun we'll have!" she said. Then to Thorn, "You'll think me a foolish and superstitious woman, but sometimes I think you were sent by some mysterious force just when we needed you."

Thorn smiled, but he didn't say anything right away. He stood where he was and it seemed to Jenny the kitchen got darker, but it was probably just the effect of the sun climbing higher in the sky outside and the thickness of Land's End's walls that made the room more shadowed.

Finally Thorn said, "Placed in your path by destiny." His voice had dropped low as it had the night before when he had spoken to Jenny, and the words seemed to come as a whisper across the distance between them.

Inadvertently Jenny reached out again and almost put her arm about Cassie once more but Thorn looked directly at her and she dropped her arm, sure that he knew that she had felt Cassie needed protection.

But it was Cassie who changed the mood of the moment. She looked at Thorn and then at Jenny and she said, in what had to be the worst moment of Jenny's life, "You two children are so beautiful."

Jenny wanted to drop right through the floor into the dusty spaces of the old winecellar.

"Cassie!" she protested and to her horror, the blood started to rise in her neck.

"Well, you are, you know," Cassie said, laughing at Jenny's confusion. "I think beauty is a gift from the gods, and it's really very silly not to enjoy it if you have it. I always did," she added, raising her chin defiantly.

By now Thorn was smiling broadly, and though she would have died on the rack rather than admit it, the full voltage of that white, uneven smile caught Jenny as it had yesterday and, coming on the heels of Cassie's outrageous comment, made her feel awkward and shy as she hadn't in a long time.

Cindy was always saying that Jenny was so "together" that she was inhuman. Jenny knew that was so partially because Cassie had always been so scatterbrained that she'd had to grow up faster in many ways than other children. But if Cindy had seen Jenny today, shifting awkwardly from foot to foot and looking at her hands as though they had sprouted in the last ten minutes, she would have seen an entirely different Jenny.

Jenny, for one thing, now knew why the stories she had read in newspapers about children in North Dakota strangling their grandmothers were possible. These two awkward hands that she didn't know what to do with wanted to reach out and shake Cassie hard.

How could she have said such a thing? If Cassie had very firm rules about not asking personal questions in case you embarrassed someone, she had very loose rules for herself about what she said. Most of the time she said whatever came into her mind.

"I'll bet you gave the men a terrible time,". Thorn was teasing Cassie.

"I was never a flirt," she said laughing, "but I always loved attention. Everybody loves attention," Cassie said wickedly, looking slyly at Jenny.

Jenny had another thought that perhaps she could drop Cassie into the cellar below, preferably on her head.

And then Thorn came to Jenny's rescue, saying, "Would you like to come out and see the garden?" His voice had done another of his rapid switches, and now he was a shy, small boy in a big strong body.

In any case, if the Hunchback of Notre Dame had walked in and invited Jenny to come swing on the bellrope that moment, she would have accepted to escape the situation. "Sure," she said, moving so fast that she was half out the door before Cassie shouted, "I'm going to town—do you want me to bring something back?"

"A gag for a grandmother if you see one!" Jenny shouted, and heard Thorn laughing behind her as he closed the kitchen door.

4

Outside, a smell of warm earth and peat moss came from behind the hawthorn hedges. Jenny turned her face into the sun. A cloud of blue and yellow butterflies billowed past on the soft summer air. "Paradise," she murmured, hugging herself about the arms.

"Close to it," Thorn said quietly behind her.

She opened her eyes to look at him. Outside he looked, not ordinary, certainly not that. He was still as beautiful as ever but . . . she searched for the right word. He looked *comfortable*, not frightening as he had for a moment there in the cool shadows of the kitchen. Outside he looked . . . she had it. "You look like the All-American boy," she said with a smile. "You look . . ." she found the exact word ". . . wholesome."

He squinched up his face. "Ugh," he said. "Wholesome?" He pretended to be hurt. "What about . . ." He struck a pose, squaring his shoulders, holding a rake like a spear. "Bold?"

"Wholesome," Jenny said, shaking her head.

"Dashing?" he bargained.

She wouldn't be budged. "Wholesome," she insisted.

He shrugged, puffing out his cheeks with a sigh. "I guess I'll have to settle for that," he said. "I was thinking that you were . . ."

He started to walk toward the vegetable garden.

"Were what?" Jenny asked, hurrying after him.

He looked at her and kept on walking, shaking his head. "I don't know if I should say it," he said.

"Say *what?*" she asked.

"Well . . ." he began.

"Thorn, you stop right where you are, if you value your life!" Jenny said, jumping in front of him. She had jumped closer than she intended because he was still walking. Her face was almost pressed to his T-shirt. She could smell the odor of what Cassie's father would have called "good hard labor." Her mind seemed to do a little spin at the closeness of Thorn, but now she'd made her stand, she couldn't jump back.

He was looking right down on her as he spoke, "I was thinking you were"—he paused for effect—"very . . . very *attractive.*"

Jenny stepped back. "That's *it?*" she asked, disappointed.

He raised his shoulders in a mock shrug, "Oh, and that you had . . .", another pause, "a nice *personality.*"

Jenny took a deep breath. "A nice personality?" she asked warningly. "You thought I was *attractive* and had a nice *personality?*"

He nodded, his face as smooth as a pebble, expressionless.

"Attractive, and a nice personality," Jenny said, "are the words you use to sucker someone into a blind date."

She wasn't sure, but she thought that the corners of his mouth twitched. "With a boy who was *wholesome?*" he asked innocently.

Jenny smiled. "Pretty boring couple, huh?" she asked.

"The lowest," he said.

Neither of them spoke for a few seconds. They stood two feet away assessing each other. Jenny listened to the bees humming in the honeysuckle over the kitchen door.

"Truce?" Thorn asked.

She couldn't help it. Despite all her suspicions, she liked him. She knew why Cassie had been such a victim of his All-American outdoorsy charm. She made a small mental note to herself not to be too taken in, but then she laughed and said, "Truce."

Together they turned and went on through the gate in the hawthorn hedge toward the vegetable garden. When she saw it, Jenny felt she had to sit down, though she didn't. "We're meant to look after *this?*" she asked weakly.

The old vegetable garden had been expanded into a patch the size of a small field.

"No use planning too little, if we expect to make money," Thorn said. "Got to make a profit."

"But this?" Jenny said gesturing at row upon row of neat furrows, some of them already furred with an early growth of crops: radishes, tiny lacy carrot tops, the snaking vines of potato plants. A square of teepeed poles in the far distance hinted at beans to be grown, and Jenny thought the first spearing blades of leaves in the last two rows might be corn.

"We can do it," Thorn said simply.

"All Cassie and I ever did," Jenny said, "was plant a small patch enough for the two of us."

"I know how to do it," Thorn reassured her seriously. "I know all about farming."

Jenny thought then that that was probably part of the answer she had been searching for all morning. She had been right in her guess. He was an All-American boy, probably from some farm. He had no accent she could pick up, but now her imagination conjured up a farmhouse, a mother, a father, maybe six or eight children, a good wholesome family with enough love and food to go around, but not enough money for a college education or any of the things Jenny and her friends thought important.

But Thorn had that something extra—curiosity about what was out there beyond the horizon, so he'd wandered, searching, she was sure, for his own answers.

She liked him suddenly. "Okay, General," she said simply. "Lead on." She picked up the hoe that he had placed nearby. He smiled at her and she knew he liked her, too, and that, for some reason, made her feel happy. He didn't move, but when the moment had dragged on until it was almost uncomfortable, he sort of swallowed, and taking a deep breath, said, "Uh . . ."

Jenny waited. But when he spoke, he said the last thing she would have expected him to say.

"Uh . . ." he said again, "do you think an attractive girl with a good personality would . . . uh . . ."

She knew what was coming now, but when he paused too long, her heart started to race, and she was suddenly afraid he wouldn't finish.

"Would what?" she asked, and to her surprise, her voice cracked.

But Thorn didn't notice. His eyes were locked on hers, and now Jenny was feeling very strange. Later she would think it had been the sun, but standing there waiting for him to finish, she felt weak and well, not quite normal, nauseous almost.

"Do you think she'd be interested in going to a movie with a wholesome boy?" he said in a rush.

The sigh Jenny gave made both of them laugh. Thorn was the one who should have been sighing, having got that out finally, but it was Jenny who was relieved.

"Oh, I think so," she said, regaining some of her composure.

"Really?" he asked, the drop-dead smile breaking across his face.

"Sure," she said, surprised.

After that they worked in the garden. Thorn did the heavy work, hauling the new peat to fertilize the rows and Jenny went down the rows thinning out the new plants until she thought that her back was permanently bent in a stooping position. Cassie came back from town, bringing the lengths of perforated hose that Thorn needed to set up an automatic sprinkling system. Then she made sandwiches and cold lemonade for them all and brought it out to the small gazebo.

Thorn went off to the side, stripped off his T-shirt and ran the cold hose over his head and chest to wash himself down. When he came back, he was wearing a clean blue shirt and had his hair neatly combed.

Cassie caught the quiet mood of Jenny and Thorn. She set out a red and white checked table cloth and put the sandwiches in front of each of them. Thorn lay sprawled on the grass at the entrance to the gazebo, eating his cheese and tomato sandwich while Jenny looked out across the dunes to where the gulls glided over the silver surface of the afternoon sea. Once she looked back she saw Cassie looking inland toward Land's End. The afternoon sun made the worn brick walls blush with a soft rose light, and she thought how sad it was that Cassie would have to leave all this one day. She was glad in almost the same moment that Thorn had been sent to them to give Cassie one last, lovely summer in her old home.

Jenny looked at Thorn then and he was dozing, his face in her shadow and his long body stretched out near the steps of the gazebo. Asleep he looked as innocent as a child, and she couldn't help wondering once more what his own home had been like and how he had come here.

When he did wake up, he did so slowly, stretching while he was still half asleep, moaning a few words that neither Jenny nor Cassie—looking at each other inquiringly—understood. His eyes opened, and he stared at each of them. A look of panic passed through the depths of his eyes. Then he blinked and brought that special smile, tentatively at first, then with more assurance back to his face.

"Got to work," he said, standing up. He was dizzy with sleep and the dream that had woken him.

Cassie and Jenny watched him go off toward the vegetable garden without a word.

Jenny helped clean up the debris from the picnic, tied it up in the red checkered cloth and started back toward the house beside Cassie. As they went past the vegetable garden, she had a glimpse of Thorn hard at work again, laying out the hose along the rows, and remembered suddenly that he had asked her to a movie.

Maybe she would learn more about him then.

5

Jenny breathed in the soft evening air as Thorn drove Cassie's yellow Buick through the back roads. "You know your way around," she said.

He looked at her, one hand lightly on the mahogany steering wheel, the other draped casually behind her on the worn leather seat. "I like to know my neighborhood," he said with a smile.

He had a haircut. He looked younger. Tonight he wore a very old light blue sweater that Jenny recognized as having been expensive, from one of the big stores in New York or maybe Boston or Los Angeles. She wondered if he'd been given it, perhaps by another boy who was older and had outgrown it. Under the sweater he wore a white button-down shirt with a frayed collar that didn't look at all shabby on him. With his jeans and his loafers, he looked like every girl's dream, she thought, and she wondered why she was so comfortable with him. She'd only known him a week, yet she found she could talk to Thorn as she couldn't to most boys.

Once in a while as they worked together in the garden and around the house, some of the old suspicions had risen in her mind, but she had rejected them as unworthy. Thorn was Thorn, and she had to admit that she had come to like him the way Cassie did.

"You're smart," she told him. "Soon the summer people will be here and then the main highway will be jammed. You can always tell the locals because we know all the back roads. We scurry along the lanes like busy little field mice while the summer people sit dead on the highway waiting for a break in the traffic."

They had come to the Sagaponack bridge over the marsh. An old man sat in the still of the early summer night with a fishing pole stuck over the water as it ran through the narrow passage under the bridge. Jenny watched the paler shadow of two swans as they floated upstream. "Do you ever want to just freeze life at one moment?" she asked.

The car bumbled gently over the wooden struts of the bridge. "No," he said.

"You don't?" Jenny asked surprised. "You never thought that everything was perfect, and you wanted the world to stop right there?"

"No," he said simply. Then they drove up the slope beyond the bridge. He drove on for a few more minutes before he turned to her with his radiant smile and said, "I'm an optimist. I always expect things to get better. That's what Cassie and I have in common."

The lights of Southampton glowed in the distance as they came out onto the highway near the entrance to the town. Jenny saw that a new hamburger franchise had erected an arch that rainbowed gold and red in the night. "I get sad sometimes," she said, "at all the changes. Cassie is much better at changes than I am. In some ways I think Cassie is *younger* than I am; does that make sense?"

"Knowing Cassie, it does," he said.

Jenny felt she was floating through a dream. A new moon hung over the water as they turned down the main street. On each side they passed white, ghostly houses afloat on smooth silver lawns.

"Where are you from?" she asked Thorn abruptly. She hadn't known she was going to, but suddenly she felt that it was unfair that she knew so little about him. He knew almost everything about her, and she knew nothing about him.

He slowed the car to let a group of six teenagers pass in front of it. For a moment she thought that he might not answer at all. He seemed to be considering. "Does it matter?" he asked.

"No," she said, "but everybody's from somewhere."

He sighed. "I don't want to be from anywhere," he said. "I just want to be Thorn."

The town opened up right there into the main

shopping center. Thorn took his time finding a parking place and put the cherished yellow convertible, Cassie's pride, neatly into the space. He walked around and opened the door for Jenny.

Her good mood of a few minutes ago was waning. He had rebuked her, avoided her question very neatly, but now, as though he knew what she was thinking, he took her arm and whispered, "Somewhere a long way away."

The night was too perfect for her to hold her bad mood long.

"How far away?" she asked.

"The South," he said.

"You don't sound as though you were from the South," she said. "My mother was a schoolteacher," he said. "She made me practice until I lost my accent. She thought it 'lower class' to have an accent." He looked down at her and flashed that bright smile, a smile that for Jenny dimmed the light of the moon. "She'd be real proud of me tonight. She'd say I was doing right fine tonight," he said letting a southern cracker accent break through his normally accentless speech.

They were coming to the old movie house. In the summer when the tourists and the summer people arrived, the movie house was full every night, but the rest of the year the theater was half empty. Tonight Jenny recognized some of the local youngsters, children she had seen every year of her life. She realized that she hardly knew them except to smile and say hello and they hardly knew her. They lived here all year but she went away to school, and when she was back, she always lived at Land's End, the biggest house on the dunes, money or no money.

She felt closer to Thorn than ever and said, "I think that's so strange that your mother would worry about accents. I don't think money and all that makes much difference to you?"

He was fumbling in his jeans for some cash. Jenny hastily opened her own bag and started to offer him money but the look that crossed his face, part hurt, part anger, stopped her. He bought their tickets and they went inside the ratty old theater. She liked the way he didn't ask her where she wanted to sit but led them down the aisle and then right to the two seats in the exact center of the theater. When they had settled in their seats, he said, "That's because you've never had to go without anything." "It's always people with money who think money doesn't make a difference. If you asked any person who was poor, they'd tell you it makes a big difference." His voice was flat and calm, not angry, but coming to her through the darkness as the lights dimmed and the movie began.

Later when she tried to think about it, she realized that she didn't really know what the movie was about. The dimming lights robbed her of Thorn right at the moment when he was ready to talk. She wanted to take his hand and rush him up the aisle, out into the summer night and drive in Cassie's yellow convertible down to the beach and talk. She wanted him to tell her about his mother who was a schoolteacher and his father. She wanted to know if he had any brothers and sisters and what the town was like where he had grown up. She wanted to know all that and much more, but the screen lit up right then and the movie began.

Thorn slid down, bracing his knees against the back of the empty seat in front. The light from the screen made planes of his cheekbones as he narrowed his eyes to concentrate on the story. Jenny tried not to stare, forcing herself to watch the action on the screen, but her mind wandered off along its own mysterious paths as it often did. She was famous at school for staring blankly at people after they had stopped talking. Something they had said half-way through their own speech had triggered other thoughts in Jenny and she stopped listening.

At some point in the movie, Thorn moved, shifting his weight so that he was sitting up. He put his arm about Jenny as naturally as though they had been going out together for years and settled her against his shoulder. Her first impulse was to resist, thinking that he was taking too much for granted, but the feeling of his shoulder behind her neck and his arm about her sent a warm feeling all through her and then, worse, she thought of Cindy and how envious she would be if she could see Jenny right now snuggled into the crook of the shoulder of this tall, blond All-American boy with the mysterious past. She could feel the rough wool of his sweater against her cheek and smell the clean scent of soap and shampoo that came from him.

He'll turn soon and kiss me. The thought ran through her mind as loud as though she had spoken it. No one had ever kissed her. Her mind went blank at the thought of Thorn turning his head and placing his lips on hers and she lost track of the movie. She was half afraid and half excited, and she thought he must know that she was tense because she couldn't move her body. She stared straight ahead with her eyes open, but she wasn't seeing anything that was on the screen.

Once Thorn shifted his arm on her shoulder, and his head moved slightly as he adjusted his neck along the back of the seat. Jenny thought this was the moment when he'd make his move. Her throat closed with fear and she croaked out a strange sound that was a cross between "E" and "Nooo." But all Thorn did was turn his head and look at her strangely and ask, "Are you all right?"

"Swallowed wrong," she managed to choke out without having to look back at him. His head was just a few inches from her face, and if she turned, they'd be eye to eye.

She thought and thought and thought about what her first kiss would be like. Cindy and she had discussed at length where the best place would be and who the best boy would be. Yet when you got right down to it, Jenny figured, sitting there beside Thorn as stiff with fear as a rabbit that saw a snake in the grass, this moment would be hard to beat: A summer town, a boy like a god, a half-deserted theater.

Yet if he did kiss her, she knew she would leap four feet straight in the air with fear and the whole theater would laugh and that would be how she would remember her first kiss for the rest of her life.

Life is ridiculous, Jenny thought. Life is disorganized. What life really needed was a good director.

But all Thorn did was squeeze her shoulder and lean over slightly and rest his own head near her shoulder and slowly the movie came back into focus for Jenny. The lights came up soon after and Thorn applauded the credits. Then they went out into the quiet of the summer night.

Thorn stood there with his hands in his jeans looking up and down the empty street.

"Remind you of home?" Jenny asked. She hadn't meant anything special, but the way he was standing there with a sort of sad look on his face as the movie emptied of the last people and the lights went off abruptly on the marquee, she thought he might be homesick.

Thorn scowled. "What?"

"I thought probably every town looked like this?" Jenny said, feeling awkward.

He looked up and down the street. He relaxed. "Yeah," he said vaguely. "I guess so."

The lights in the ice cream stand at the end of the street caught his attention. "What type of ice cream do you like?" he said.

"Peach," Jenny said without hesitation.

"Peach?" He scowled. "What type of person likes peach ice cream?"

51

"Peach is the best," Jenny said flatly.

He winced. "What type of hick are you?" he asked her. "You must have lived a real sheltered life. You ever tasted pistachio?"

Jenny put her hand to her throat. "Pistachio?" She gagged. She stuck out her tongue and bulged her eyes.

"Into the car," he ordered her, opening the door.

Jenny allowed herself to be helped into the car, visibly weakened at the thought of pistachio ice cream.

Silently, as though in the presence of a lunatic, he got in behind the wheel and solemnly drove them to the ice cream stand. Without a word he stood in line and waited his turn at the window.

When he returned, Jenny sighed heavily. "I hope that's not pistachio," she said looking at the bag.

Thorn backed the car out of the parking lot and drove them quietly back along the main highway. As they turned in the driveway of Land's End, he said, "There comes a time in every young woman's life when she has to learn about life."

Jenny was laughing. "And life is a taste for pistachio ice cream?" she asked.

"Don't joke about this," Thorn said. "This is one of the most important moments of your life."

"Sorry," Jenny said, holding back her laughter.

He doused the lights as they came up the driveway and cut the engine so as not to wake Cassie. The yellow Buick slowed by its own momentum to a halt by the front terrace. Thorn got out, carrying the package. He opened the door for Jenny and closed it softly behind her. He took her hand and without words led her across the moonlit lawn toward the silhouetted roofline of the boathouse at the edge of the water.

Jenny's heart began to beat faster and she wanted suddenly to pull back and run back to the house, but she was afraid that if she did so, Thorn would laugh at her. Her breath was coming in smaller gasps and as the dark bulk of the boathouse rose out of the marsh's edge, she felt her heart hammering so hard in her ribcage that she was sure he must hear it.

She was going to break away and run when he turned away from the boathouse and led her out on the small dock that thrust into the creek where it fed from the marsh into the waters of the sound. He put the package on the dock, stripped off his sweater in one movement, and just as Jenny was about to turn away again, laid it at her feet with a gesture for her to sit down.

Her knees seemed to collapse under her. Before she knew it, she was sitting down on the dock looking at the gentle current as it moved through the water. Jenny lost track of her thoughts for a second, then Thorn was sitting beside her, his legs crossed and the package in his lap. He opened it and looked at her with a smile that caught the moonlight. His eyes were bright as they met hers, and she was smiling back against her will. Her fear drained and she felt grateful to him for no reason could understand. He raised his hands, palms out, and in each was a small carton of ice cream.

"Pistachio," he whispered, holding one palm into the light of the moon.

And then raising the other, "Peach."

Jenny was filled with such happiness she wanted to leap forward and kiss him, and she had no good reason for that either.

"I like my ice cream melted," he said in the same soft voice. "You?"

"Melted," she whispered back. "Is there any other way?"

Then he produced two plastic spoons and they each took their own carton of ice cream. Jenny thought as she tasted the first soft mouthful of peach that this must be the best moment of her life.

They sat there and ate their ice cream without saying a word until the spoon scraped on the bottom of her carton. She knew Thorn was there beside her but she had also let her mind slip away for a moment. Now she came back to the present to find him watching her with those bright, long-lashed eyes.

He leaped forward and placed his lips on hers. Time stopped and raced forward at the same time and she knew what all this talk about love was about, because she wanted this moment to go on and on and on, and she never ever wanted to kiss anybody else for she knew, without any doubt, that she was in love with this boy who had given her her first kiss.

Slowly their lips came apart as naturally as they had gone together and they were just staring and staring at each other and she knew without a word spoken that he felt exactly the same way.

After a few seconds he leaned back and sighed. He picked up the carton of ice cream and spooned out the last of it. He held it out to her. Jenny leaned forward and took the ice cream in her mouth.

"Pistachio," he said.

She swallowed. "It's not peach," she whispered, "but I could get used to it." He sighed. "I think you're perfect," he said.

6

The fog rolled in from the ocean. "Sometimes," Thorn said, holding Jenny against him, "I look at Land's End and I see a palace, a palace like in a fairy tale."

Jenny lay against Thorn's chest. From the boathouse they watched the light in Cassie's window, silver against the red brick of Land's End.

"And the princess is in her tower," she said.

"The queen is in her tower," Thorn corrected her. He brushed his lips across the top of Jenny's head. "The princess isn't home yet."

A small chill crept across Jenny's heart. She said, "Thorn, what will happen when the summer is over?"

Thorn didn't reply. Jenny waited and then looked up at his face. When he was thinking, his eyes would partly close and his lips press hard on each other.

"I don't want to talk about that," he said.

A shadow passed in front of Cassie's window and Jenny thought she could see a small figure looking out across the lawn. "The house won't sell, will it?" she asked quietly.

Thorn pressed her against him slightly. "All fairy tales have happy endings," he said, "you know that."

"But this is real life," Jenny reminded him.

His sigh escaped him like a breath. "Not tonight," he said, looking at the sickle moon's silvered path on the roof of Land's End. "Not today, not this summer."

Jenny wanted to talk, but she knew that in one way Thorn was right. This wasn't real life here at Land's End. Not just because Thorn was there. Life out here on the edge of the land with the old house and the gardens all about it had never been real life. She had known that for a long time. Even when the house was falling down, it was like a fairy tale, a fairy tale in which a sleeping kingdom with a spell cast on it had been slowly taken back by the creeping brambles and the weeds, waiting for its prince.

And then one day Thorn had come.

"What will you do after the summer?" Jenny asked him, feeling her heart contract as she did so.

A chill draft hissed under the door of the boathouse. Jenny shivered. "You'll go away, won't you?" she said.

Thorn's answer was to hug her closer. She felt the soft wool of his sweater against her cheek, and her eyes seemed to half close of their own will. She wanted to fall asleep against his chest, listening to the soft murmur of his heartbeat. Thorn had become as familiar to her as Cassie.

She wasn't sure at first that she had heard him, for his voice was a whisper. "I want to spend the rest of my life with you," his voice said.

Jenny's heart stopped for a fraction of a second, then raced on.

"That's what I would like to do," he said, his voice a soft rustle of breath above her head.

She leaned back and looked up at him. She loved Thorn as she had never thought she would ever love anyone. She loved him in a way quite unlike the way she loved Cassie. And everything she had ever read about love had been true. She felt complete with Thorn. She trusted him and felt natural and free with him, and when he was away, she felt a loss as though part of her body was missing and she wasn't calm again until he was back.

She knew that Cassie was thinking, too, because she saw the way Cassie looked at her with concern in her eyes. She saw the way Cassie's glance went from Jenny to Thorn but they had never discussed it.

She said something instead that she knew was unfair. "I think I would die if you went away now."

Thorn shuddered, then he tried to cover it up by holding her tighter. "I won't go away," he said.

"I could work and you could go to school," Jenny offered.

Now Thorn laughed at her, softly, and then he kissed her on the temple. "Where is all the women's liberation now?" he said. "What would be the difference if I got an education or if you did? I can have a trade and you can go to school. I like to work with my hands."

"But it seems so unfair," Jenny said. "You're so smart. You should be able to go to college."

"Going to college isn't everything," he said evenly. "I don't think a person has to go to college to be someone in this world."

That wasn't what Jenny had meant. But the day her own acceptance to college had arrived at Land's End with the announcement that she had won a scholarship, she had seen Thorn's face as Jenny and Cassie had rejoiced in the good news. Thorn had stood by and he had looked thoughtful. It had been a long moment before he leaned forward and kissed Jenny gently on the cheek and said, "Congratulations. I'm happy for you."

The moment had lost some of its excitement, but Thorn wouldn't let Jenny play down the importance of the acceptance and he had suddenly swung an arm about both Cassie and Jenny and said, "My treat. We're going out." He had taken them both down to the seafood restaurant in the next town where few tourists went. There they had had lobster and fresh corn, and Cassie had sprung for a bottle of house wine. When the three of them were driving back crammed in the front seat of the old yellow Buick, they had all felt giddy and silly. Thorn had suddenly started to sing in a deep baritone that startled Cassie and Jenny. He had sung negro spirituals and his voice had rolled out across the marshes as they passed them. Cassie and Jenny were silent listening to him.

"Where did you learn those songs?" Cassie asked as the car crunched to a halt on the gravel drive outside Land's End.

"At home," Thorn said.

Cassie had looked at him long and hard. "I always liked southern boys," she said. "They have manners." She'd leaned across Jenny and kissed Thorn, touching his cheek. "You're a good boy, Thorn," she said. Then she leaped out of the car and said, "And I'm a sentimental and silly old woman who needs her rest."

Cassie had rushed into the house and left the two youngsters alone in the car.

Maybe it was the little bit of wine they had been allowed at dinner; maybe it was the night with the stars flung across the black sky; maybe it was the sound of the waves thundering in across the sand with the force of a coming storm; maybe it was the songs that he had sung to Cassie and Jenny on the way home, but Thorn had talked that night to Jenny for the first time about his past.

They walked arm in arm down to the beach and he had said, "Life should be simple shouldn't it? A person should need someone special, and a place to live and work he likes. That's all you should need, isn't it?"

They came to the tips of the dunes and stood watching the water foam fiercely up the beach. Clouds scudded across the moon and the wind came in off the ocean and blew Jenny's hair across her face.

"People make life difficult."

"Yes," he agreed. "But there are an awful lot of people in this world and just two of us."

Jenny thought suddenly of Cindy who would be coming to visit in a week and wondered if Cindy was still keeping her list of all the people she had met in her life.

She hoped Cindy and Thorn liked each other, since Cindy was Jenny's best friend. If Cindy and Thorn liked each other, life would be perfect, Jenny thought.

Jenny had been about to talk about Cindy when Thorn said, "When I was growing up I used to think that I would never, ever be able to be grown up." He looked at her. "Did you?"

"No," Jenny said, "I assumed that growing up just happened. You didn't do anything about it."

"You want to sit down?" Thorn asked gesturing at the rough dune grass. They sat huddled together out of the wind and he said, "Oh, that, yeah, I knew people got older and all, but you know I used to wonder about how I would ever make a living and meet someone special and have a family and I would

61

look around at all these grownups and it just . . . it just seemed so complicated. I didn't figure I'd ever be able to do it."

"But you did," Jenny said. And then added, "or part of it. I mean you make a living, you're real independent. And . . ."

"And I met someone special," he said.

Jenny wanted to ask more. But she knew that Thorn had already opened up more than he liked to. "And you'll figure out the rest," she finally said. "I know you will."

After that they had talked about their childhoods. Thorn knew all about Jenny's. All he had to do was look around. But he told her now that he had grown up in the South as Cassie had guessed, that his mother had died when he was very young and that he had been raised by another woman, a black woman who taught him the songs he had sung that night. He didn't talk about his father, and he didn't say anything about the house he had lived in. Jenny didn't ask. She thought there would be other times when he would fill in all the little details that she wanted to know, about his school and his friends and what his room had looked like, but she thought if she asked him now he would be embarrassed to tell her because she was sure he had been very, very poor. Land's End loomed up behind them, and inside on the hall table, were the documents that had come that day saying she would be able to go on to college, while Thorn had to make his own way in the world.

And anyway she wanted the night to go on forever

with the wind in their faces and the sea stretching away endlessly in front of them, right to another continent. "If we had a boat," she suggested, "we could sail away and leave all the other people behind."

"I love you, Jenny Castle," Thorn said as they watched the fog billow about the foundations of Land's End.

"And I love you, Thorn," Jenny said.

"Then love will have to find a way," Thorn said softly.

The light went out in Cassie's window. Thorn rose and took Jenny's hand and they walked quietly side by side back to the house.

7

The summer people came. They came in sports cars and station wagons, by train and by jitney, they came by seaplane to land on the quiet waters of the bay beyond the marsh and some of them even came by helicopter, flattening the leaves of the chestnut trees as the lethal blades spun around to let the little glass bubbles settle on the manicured lawns of the richest visitors.

"Man," Thorn said, looking at the traffic stopped dead at the intersection into Bridgehampton. They were bringing some of their Land's End produce to market. "This is the craziest thing I ever saw. Back where I come from this only happens at the Fourth of July picnic. Fourth of July, whole county heads for the lake. Biggest blowout you ever saw, fireworks, hot dogs, home baked pies. You meet everybody you ever knew at the Fourth of July picnic."

When he spoke like that Thorn dropped into an accent, soft, and hard to pin down, but different from his regular speech.

"It didn't used to be like this," Jenny said. "Back when Cassie was young and great-grandfather built Land's End, it took a whole day to get out here. The family closed up the house on Fifth Avenue on the last day of May and great-grandfather moved into his club. It took three railroad cars to bring the family out to Land's End. The family rode in the first car and the house servants came in the second. The third was used for the luggage."

As she spoke, Jenny realized that she might be making Thorn feel uncomfortable. She didn't really think of those long ago days as having anything to do with herself. They were times that Cassie had told her about like fairy tales read late at night of beautiful palaces and princesses and kings who ruled distant lands.

Land's End for Jenny was just a lovable old house, too big for the family and falling further and further apart as the overgrown gardens crept closer and closer, like a jungle waiting to cover the old house and let it lie forgotten in a hundred years sleep.

"But that was all a long time ago," Jenny said lamely as the traffic began to edge inch by inch toward the flagpole at the end of the village.

Thorn said, "Must be nice to be rich, don't you think?"

Jenny thought of Cindy trailing after her mother from one expensive resort to another. "Maybe," she said.

Thorn looked at her. "You wouldn't want to be rich if you could?" he asked. His eyes were sparkling brightly at some private thought.

"If I could be rich in my own way," Jenny said carefully.

Right then a bright purple Mercedes sports car with its horn honking pulled out from behind the old Buick. It tore onto the grassy edge of the pavement and impatiently shot down the line of stalled cars toward the crossroads. Behind the wheel a man with a thick neck and a heavy gold chain leaned forward shouting obscenities at the traffic.

"Not like that," Thorn said as the purple Mercedes careened off the pavement and shot in between two vans as they made their way around the flagpole and out onto the highway toward East Hampton.

"No," Jenny admitted, thinking of what Cassie would have had to say at the sight of the Mercedes pushing ahead of everyone else. "Would you like to be rich?"

Thorn smiled. The traffic was moving smoothly now. He put the Buick in gear with the lever on the steering wheel and let out the clutch. "Me, I'm too dumb to be rich," Thorn said as they went around the flagpole, throwing Jenny gently against Thorn's side. Thorn put his arm out and over Jenny's shoulders. "Me, I'm just a country boy. Rich for me is a roof over my head, food in the cupboard and a girl by my side."

The car ahead had pulled away. Jenny settled against Thorn. His shirt was warm from the sun, soft from lots of washings. "You're not dumb, Thorn. Don't say that," she said.

"Dumbest thing a person can do," he said, letting the car settle into a nice slow speed on the highway, "is think they're better than they are. Me, I know my limits. Back home I saw all sorts of people filled with jealousy because other people were rich or had better clothes or prettier girls. I saw all sorts of people eating themselves away with jealousy like cancer so they couldn't even enjoy what they did have. I saw that and decided that wasn't for me. 'Know thyself'," he said, looking down at Jenny with his bright eyes, "'know thyself'."

Jenny leaned back to look up at him. "That's from Shakespeare," she said.

"True?" he asked.

"Did you study Shakespeare?" she asked him.

"Must have, I guess," he said with his secret smile. "Don't remember now, but I guess I must have if you say it's from Shakespeare. Think maybe it was in a big blue book."

"Hamlet," Jenny said suspiciously.

"Whatever," Thorn said, looking ahead on the highway. "Big book of poetry now that you make me think about it. Big blue poetry book. True anyway, isn't it?"

"Yes," Jenny admitted, letting her suspicions that

Thorn might be putting her on drift away with the smell of the warm earth baking in the afternoon sun. "You could go to college, Thorn," she said. "There are student loans and stuff."

Thorn said nothing for a while. They passed off the highway, turning left into the shade of a lane of chestnut trees. "I like life simple," Thorn said finally.

Jenny knew enough of him by now not to try to draw him out any further. He had two moods, she knew well now. The one that began with the slow, secret smile that seemed to light up everyone around him and fill them with an infectious joy, and this other, moody and withdrawn. She thought when he was moody, he was thinking about his past, and Cassie had brought her up to respect people's privacy.

She still wondered where he was from. Sometimes he would talk, as he had today, about his hometown, but always vaguely, never giving it a name. He knew everything about her. All he had to do was look around. But she knew almost nothing about him.

The cool row of chestnut trees widened into open road with the fields stretching away on either side. Jenny was blinded for a moment. She closed her eyes to accustom them to the light. When she opened them Thorn was humming a tune, something she didn't recognize. He drove with one elbow resting on the door and his other hand resting lightly on the wheel. He tapped out a rhythm on the wooden steering wheel.

They turned a corner and some of the produce that was stacked high in wicker baskets on the backseat shifted. Jenny turned to stop the movement. She was still astonished that they had been able to grow so much; heads and heads of lettuce, beautiful, red luscious tomatoes, dusty healthy potatoes. Their produce already had a name up and down the highway at the open vegetable stalls. "Land's End vegetables," the owners of the stalls called it and they got just a little better than top dollar for everything they grew. Cassie was thrilled. Thorn would just smile that famous smile when he brought back the cash twice a week from delivering the vegetables.

The money was enough to keep on fixing up the garden, paint the old boathouse and start in on the paths that led through the brew hedges to the rose garden. Already Cassie had volunteered to loan Land's End for the big hospital charity fete at the end of the summer. That was the way it used to be. Land's End was open to the public one day a year for the fete that was held in the gardens. Now with the gardens again looking so fine, Cassie had agreed to hold the fete at the house one last time.

They passed close to the marshland that drained through a narrow stream near Land's End to the sea. The bulrushes stood tall in the sunlight while ducks upended themselves searching for delicious things to eat on the bottom of the marsh.

"Birds have the right idea," Thorn said suddenly. "They make their houses in the lakes and trees. They come to the shore in the summer and go south in the winter. I bet ducks don't worry about who's got the biggest house and the newest Mercedes. I bet a duck wouldn't pay eight dollars for a strawberry pie the way I saw some guy pay yesterday in that new little store in town."

"I imagine all worms cost about the same," Jenny agreed with amusement.

"Every duck has to work for his own food; that's what you mean," Thorn said.

Jenny understood what Thorn was getting at. Here in the summer people lost all sense of proportion. Some people seemed to have so much money they almost *liked* to pay too much for things. She would hear people on the street laughing at the ridiculous prices, but they paid them anyway.

"Not everybody's like that," Jenny said. "Cassie used to be rich and she's not like that and she wouldn't be even if she was rich again."

But Thorn had withdrawn into one of his quiet moods when she knew the best thing to do was leave him alone. So she sat in the far corner of the seat and thought her own thoughts. She was a good student and she had already won a scholarship to college. She wished there was some way Thorn could go to college too. She know how he must feel seeing all these summer people waste their money.

They were coming to one of their best customers, Danny's Roadside Produce, a long series of tumbledown shacks at the side of the highway. Danny was a local man whose wife ran the diner off to the side.

Both Danny and his wife loved Thorn. Lots of people loved Thorn, Jenny thought. Thorn got along with people well. He won their respect by his manner and his easy good humor, and Jenny always felt proud to be with him.

"Hey, Thorn," Danny called as the old Buick stopped. "What you got today?" Danny came out from behind the counter of the stand wiping his hands on his overalls. The stand was piled with bright red tomatoes, yellow corn, green beans, rust potatoes.

"Doesn't look as though you need much," Thorn said ruefully, hauling out the baskets of produce from the back seat.

"Always need your stuff," Danny said. "You've got something special. Must be in your hands. Real farm hands, I guess; you make the land give the best it's got, right?"

The way Danny looked at Thorn was almost hero worship, Jenny thought. It was the effect Thorn had on a lot of people.

"Guess so, Danny," Thorn said. "But now you talk of it, I guess I should say that since this is the best produce in the area and you know it, then maybe we should talk a little short price . . ."

And he got away with that, too, by breaking out the famous smile so that Danny just sighed and called "Mary!" Danny's wife, Mary, came out of the diner wiping her hands on her apron.

"Thorn's about to rob us again," Danny said, but Jenny could see that Danny really liked this down-home bargaining that Thorn did. "You better bring us out some coffee."

Mary waved and went back in the diner. When she came out she hung the CLOSED sign on the door. "Coffee break," she said, and she carried a tray of coffee and hot buns over to the shade near the last of the shacks.

They all settled down on the grass and Danny and Thorn began their good-humored haggling over the price of the fruits and vegetables from Land's End garden while Jenny and Mary exchanged glances of amusement.

Jenny loved being with Thorn. Everybody liked him. The people in their Mercedeses and Porsches whizzing by on the highway might be able to buy strawberry pies at eight dollars, but what Thorn had, nobody could buy. Thorn had charm.

8

I'm here," Cindy shrieked through the telephone line.

"Where?" Jenny asked. She was still half asleep. After she had come back into the house with Thorn, she had climbed the stairs to her bedroom and watched the ocean disappear under a white blanket of fog. A soft silence fell upon Land's End. "Then love must find a way." Thorn's words echoed in her mind. She trusted Thorn. Love would find a way even though she would have to go away to college.

"Here!" Cindy shrieked. "In Southampton."

The morning was cool with the last of the night's fog still floating outside the kitchen window. Jenny had overslept. She could see Cassie at the corner of the terrace filling the birdfeeder.

"Here?" she asked stupidly.

"Yes, you dingbat!" Cindy said. "Southampton. I got a ride on a private plane with a friend of my Dad's."

The words finally sunk in. "You're here!" Jenny shouted back down the line.

"I got in last night. We landed at La Guardia and drove out, but it was too late to call you. Come get me quick. These people are friends of my Dad's and"—Jenny could hear Cindy surreptitiously covering the mouthpiece of the telephone so she couldn't be overheard—"they are so boring I'm not going to even give them a number."

"Oh, Cindy." Jenny laughed. "Are you still doing that?"

"Of course, I'm doing that," Cindy said. "I'm going to become famous with my theory when I prove that there really are only two thousand people in the world. I tell you all I've met all summer are people I've known all my life."

A quick image of Thorn's face, tanned and serious as he kissed her good night, floated like the mist on the lawn before Jenny's face. She felt a thrill at having her own secret to tell Cindy. Usually Cindy was the one with all the news when they got together.

"Quick, girl," Cindy ordered her, "get right over here and rescue me. This whole house is done in beige. I feel myself becoming more and more beige every moment I'm with these people and as you know *I AM NOT A BEIGE PERSON!*"

Jenny took down the address and ran out into the garden. "Cassie," she called.

Cassie looked up from pruning the pots of geraniums along the terrace wall. As she approached, Jenny could smell the dry peppery smell of the dead flowers.

"Cindy's here!" Jenny said.

Cassie looked confused for a moment. "What day is it?" she asked.

"She got a ride with some friends of her dad's, so she's here early!" Jenny explained fast. "Where's Thorn?"

"He went into town with the day's sale," Cassie said. "You looked so fast asleep when I went to wake you, I hadn't the heart. He won't be back until late this afternoon."

Jenny's heart sank. "How will we get Cindy?" she asked.

"I'm afraid, darling, that she'll have to take a taxi," Cassie said, taking off her gardening gloves. Cassie was burned the color of sandpaper by the months working in the garden. Her little bright eyes sparkled like sapphires with the thought of Cindy's arrival. "Call up Omar and have him go get her."

Omar operated the year-round town taxi and Cassie had known him all her life. Cassie claimed that Omar had been old when *she* was young so he *had* to be a hundred now. If his driving was any indication of his age, then Cassie might well be right, for he wove all over the road and claimed that he didn't need glasses. All the full-time residents loved

Omar and wouldn't use any of the smarter, faster taxis that appeared each summer, but they had finally insisted that Omar keep to the back roads because he was a menace to life and limb out on the highway.

Jenny raced back inside the house, called Omar and sent him off to get Cindy. Then she called Cindy and told her that Omar was coming. "Sit in the back seat," she told Cindy, "and keep your eyes closed." She hung up giggling.

Cassie was already busy in the linen closet when Jenny went upstairs to help her make up Cindy's room. Cassie was taking out her best sheets, pure linen, as soft as kitten fur. They had been part of Cassie's own trousseau. Only Cassie's favorite guests got to sleep on the monogrammed linen sheets.

Together they aired out the room next to Jenny's, threw open the shutters and pulled off the dust covers from the bed and the arm chair in front of the cold fireplace. They laughed like schoolgirls as they made up the bed fresh for Cindy and were just fluffing up the pillows as they heard Omar's old Pontiac roll uncertainly up the driveway.

Jenny ran down the stairs and threw open the front door as a pale Cindy was getting out of the back of the ancient car. "You might have warned me," Cindy said coldly.

Omar was beaming. "All safe and delivered, Mrs. Castle," he said as Cassie came out of the house to pay him.

"Safe!" Cindy murmured to Jenny, dragging her

76

suitcase out of the back seat. "I've ridden roller coasters that were safer." Jenny giggled. "Believe it or not."

Cindy was about to answer that when she stopped in her tracks looking up at Land's End. "Oh, my," she said.

Cassie and Jenny waited for her to take in all the other improvements to the house. Cindy had come out to Land's End every year to visit Jenny for a few days, sometimes in the summer, sometimes at Christmas and each year the house had become more and more decrepit.

Cindy turned slowly, taking in the neatly weeded flower beds, the pruned trees, the weed-free driveway. "You found buried treasure," she said. "It's beautiful."

"Not buried treasure," Cassie said coyly, looking at Jenny, "but a treasure."

"Tell me," Cindy said.

Cassie cast another look sideways at Jenny. Silently they both agreed to let Cindy find out about Thorn later when he came home. "Come on inside," Jenny said, pulling Cindy's bag from her hands.

"Are you hungry?" Cassie asked.

"Famished," Cindy said. "They were definitely beige people with beige food. Breakfast was a muffin *without* butter and skim milk!" She made a face. "What's the use of being thin if you're hungry, I ask you?" No one could accuse Cindy of being too thin. If anything, she seemed to have gained a few more pounds on her plump little frame. Cindy's mother was rail-thin all the time, and Cindy was determined that she would never look like her mother.

Cassie went off to make Cindy another breakfast while Jenny and Cindy went up to Cindy's guest room. "You look wonderful!" Cindy said, stepping back to look at Jenny. "You look different!"

Jenny was bursting to tell Cindy about Thorn, but she also wanted to see Cindy's face when she first got a look at Thorn. She pretended to see something out in the garden. "Come on," she said, "let's go down and have something to eat, then go to the beach." Jenny went into her own room to change into a bathing suit. When she came out Cindy was standing wrapped in a long white terry cloth robe that went all the way to the floor. On her head she wore a wide-brimmed straw hat, and covering most of her face were huge dark glasses.

"I give up," Jenny said, "who are you?"

"The sun's bad for the skin," Cindy explained from behind the smoked glasses.

"So is chocolate," Jenny said, "if you eat all of Hershey, Pennsylvania. I sort of thought we'd go out for maybe an hour or two."

Cindy took no offense. She led off down the stairs trailing her white robe. Cindy liked Land's End more than any of her own homes. Watching her best friend drag the ridiculous white robe behind her down the old steps of Land's End, Jenny thought how wonderful it was to have someone like Cindy in her life with all her bizarre opinions and enthusiasms. Life around Cindy was never dull.

Cindy marched right across the front hall and out onto the terrace with Jenny following. They went down the steps to the lawn and off across the dunes to the beach where they found a secluded spot to lay out their towels.

Jenny lay down on her stomach and said, "Okay, tell. Every word."

Cindy hadn't uncovered so much as an inch of skin. More than that, she had pulled a tube of cream from one of the deep pockets of her robe and was slathering herself with a white ointment.

"Well," she said, "Daisy's getting married."

"Again!" The word was out before Jenny could stop herself. Daisy was Cindy's mother, but she refused to allow anyone to call her mother.

"Number four," Cindy said. "You think she'd learn."

"Who is he?" Jenny asked.

Cindy lay back, adjusted her glasses and pulled the hat close about her face. It would have taken a nuclear beam to penetrate her protection.

"His name is Jean-Claude," Cindy said. "He's a filmmaker. He's French, of course, with a name like Jean-Claude, and he makes these really obscure films about life and passion and revenge, but personally I don't think that he could know much about life if he's marrying Daisy with four strikes against her, though he probably knows a lot about passion if I know Daisy, and he's about to learn about revenge if he stays married to her long enough, since every husband has more or less wanted to drop her from a tall building without a parachute by the time he ran for his lawyer."

Cindy and her mother had an unusual friendship, and though when she talked about her mother, Cindy sometimes sounded critical, Jenny knew that Cindy really loved her mother. The problem was that Daisy was one of those women who had never really grown up and slowly Cindy was becoming the adult in their relationship while Daisy went on from year to year expecting people to take care of her.

Daisy's life was like a soap opera with every event a melodrama.

Cindy rolled on her side. "You know what I've been thinking?" she asked. "I've been thinking that men can't be too bright."

"Some of them are," Jenny said thinking of Thorn.

"I have my doubts," Cindy said. "I mean, what do we know of men, locked up in girl's schools? By the time we get out, we'll be way behind and have to take crash courses or something, but from what I see I can't understand why women haven't taken over the world centuries ago. You should see this Jean-Claude, tall, dark, handsome, smart and Daisy bats her mink eyelashes and bam! He's tripping over his own feet."

Jenny was on the verge then of blurting out her news about Thorn, but a family came by, a mother, father and three small children all shouting at the same time and Cindy shuddered. "No," she said. "I am never getting married." With that she lay on her back, wrapped herself in her robe and fell asleep after her long flight across the Atlantic.

Jenny watched her friend sleep. She was glad Cindy was here at Land's End. Cindy had never really had a real home of her own. She wandered all her life from one place to another, trailing after her mother and father. Then Jenny thought about what it would be like if Land's End were sold, how strange it would be not to have Land's End to come home to all the time and how strange it would be for Cassie not to live here at Land's End.

She rolled on her back and watched the gulls wheel above the beach, thinking how perfect the day was. Cindy, her best friend, was here and Thorn would soon be back from delivering the vegetables to all the stands along the highway. Tonight all her favorite people would be gathered safely in the shelter of Land's End.

Maybe there would be fog again tonight, and it would be warm enough to have a fire in the kitchen fireplace. They could all sit around the kitchen table, while Cassie and Jenny cooked and Thorn made his salad dressing and Cindy told her strange tales of Daisy and Daisy's friends like stories from another planet.

She meant to just close her eyes to keep the light out, but she fell asleep and when she woke the sun had sunk behind the dunes. The sky was gray with twilight and Cindy was sitting wrapped in her robe staring off across the beach to where the breakers rolled in across the sandbar.

"I would like to live here forever," Cindy said. "I think you are so lucky to have grown up here."

"We have to get back to the house," Jenny said excitedly. "Thorn will be back!" She was gathering up her belongings as she spoke.

"Thorn?" Cindy asked suspiciously.

"Oh," Jenny said. "I meant it to be a surprise. There's someone I want you to meet."

"A boy!" Cindy said.

"Come on, come on," Jenny said, wrapping the towel around her like a sarong.

"You've met a boy, and you let me lie here for three hours without telling me!" Cindy accused.

"Quick, quick!" Jenny said, hurrying Cindy across the dunes and onto the lawn.

In the distance she could see the yellow Buick parked off to the side of the terrace.

Cindy was trailing after Jenny in her white robe saying, "Some best friend! Secrets! I thought we were never going to have secrets from each other!"

But Jenny was half a dozen steps ahead of her, taking the steps to the terrace two at a time. Thorn was bent over, watering the pots of geraniums, his broad back stretching the tan fabric of his work shirt. At the sound of the girls coming up the steps, he turned slowly, his drop-dead smile breaking on his face as he took in the sight of Jenny wrapped in the towel and the figure of Cindy hurrying along behind, muffled in her long robe, with her straw hat and glasses covering most of her face.

Then his smile froze and Jenny had a horrible

moment of fear. Something was wrong. Thorn just stood there with the hose pouring water over his boots as his smile faded. From behind Jenny, Cindy's surprised voice cried, "Thornton Howerlock: number one two four eight."

Jenny's heart seemed to stop and she looked first at Thorn, then at Cindy, who had taken off her hat and her sunglasses and was standing beaming down the length of the space separating them. Thorn looked sick, his face gray under the tan and the light gone from his eyes.

Jenny fought to keep the fear from her voice as she said, "You know each other?"

"Know each other!" Cindy said, unaware of the coldness that was creeping like a frost around Jenny's heart. "Of course we know each other! Thornton Melton Howerlock, where have you been? Don't you know your daddy has half of Florida looking for you?"

9

Cindy was gone. Jenny watched the train pull away around the bend. A silence descended on the railroad station. Cassie was sitting behind the wheel of the Buick watching worriedly. When Jenny came back to the car she said, "Would you like to drive to Montauk and have lunch by ourselves?"

Jenny still felt as though her heart would break at any moment into two pieces. She knew that Cindy really didn't have an emergency that had taken her into the city to catch a plane to join her father early. Cindy was being kind. For four days, since Cindy inadvertently had let out the news that Thorn was a fake, Jenny had been shut in a private misery so deep that she could hardly speak, hardly listen, hardly eat or sleep.

"Okay," Jenny said quietly.

Cassie said nothing as they drove out of the parking lot onto the dusty highway. She found the first back road and turned off, threading her way toward the farthest point of land where the lighthouse beamed its warning to ships in winter.

Jenny felt as though she were in a dream as she watched familiar landmarks pass by. They passed the Thompson Farm, the mill that dated to the American revolution, the place where she had first learned to ride a bicycle, and always, insistently, a pain would grasp at her heart because at each of them she had memories of Thorn. She had led him to these places all summer to show them to him so he would understand where she had grown up, what had happened to her. So he would know her better.

And he had shared things with her, too, little stories of his first bicycle that had been handed down from his brother, of learning to swim in a pond with a board torn from a fence to keep him afloat, of picking berries so his mother could cook them into pies. He had never told her much, but when he did give her the little crumbs, she had seized on them as clues to his past. She had stored them away in her mind as part of him that she knew that nobody else did, for by then she was sure that his childhood had been desperately poor and painful, and he had run away from some place very young to make his own way in the world.

"I want to create myself," he had once said to her

as they watched a mother duck with a string of ducklings trailing up the calm water above the slough.

He hadn't said anything else, but knowing what she thought she did of his past, Jenny had allowed herself to believe that he meant he didn't want to be trapped by the poverty of his past.

All of that had dropped away the moment Cindy had shouted, "Thornton Howerlock the Third. One two four eight."

The world had frozen for one moment, gone quite still as though the sun itself wasn't moving. The seagulls that a moment before had been wheeling over the shallows of the incoming tide had been pinned seaward to the gray twilight backdrop of the sky.

Then the world had started again and Thorn, dead white beneath the tan, had looked at his feet where the water of the hose was pouring over his boots and taken a deep sigh that Jenny could hear from where she stood. He didn't look at her. He went and turned off the water and rolled up the hose with his back turned to them. Even Cindy, who usually missed any moods or nuances, had for once known that something was wrong. She stood in her ridiculous white robe looking from Thorn to Jenny without a word.

Jenny had thought she was about to throw up on the wet bricks of the terrace.

"Have I said something wrong?" Cindy asked finally in a voice quite unlike her own, a tiny little girl's voice, part apology, part confusion.

It was Thorn who answered. "Hi, Cindy," he said. "How was Palm Beach?"

Uncertainly Cindy looked toward Jenny. "Empty," she said in that same small voice. "I was just there a few days before we went to Europe. Daisy had left some jewelry in the bank she wanted to take with her." Her voice trailed off.

And then she said, "Your dad's half crazy looking for you."

Now Thorn looked at Jenny. A whole summer of lies must have shown in her face. She felt like a fool, and as suddenly as she had loved him, she hated Thorn in one moment.

"Jenny . . ." he said quietly.

But she turned and walked away down the terrace which seemed cruelly long, so long that she had to start running so that he wouldn't see the tears that were welling up in her eyes. She turned the corner and ran blindly down the steps to the lawn and off as fast as she could down the driveway and out onto the highway. The late summer night had shadowed the world as she found a place beneath the hedge that protected a mansion half a mile away from the eyes of the common man, the common man whom she had thought Thorn was, until a few minutes ago. She crawled under there, curled herself into a ball and allowed the cries to come out, deep cries of pain and betrayal, that wracked her body and drained the tears from her eyes, until they died in heavy choking sobs. She had fallen asleep after that and when she awoke it was to the blinding light of a sportscar going by fast on the nearby road.

She lay there a while longer, searching and trying to understand what had happened to her. She felt nothing at first. The tears and the sobs had emptied her. She was careful not to think of Thorn, and then tentatively she did, testing the intense pain she had felt when she knew that all his stories of his past, all he had allowed her to believe of his poor childhood, was a lie. If that was a lie then he had just toyed with her, used her as a little foolish girl in his own game, and the pain swept back into her and she had to close her eyes and take a deep breath.

She found that if she didn't think at all of Thorn, didn't allow his name to pass through her mind, his face to float through her memory, she could breathe normally again. She lay there practicing that for a while longer before she crawled out of her shelter and brushed the dirt from her arms and legs. She was still wearing the towel and she began to feel more than just foolish, as she hurried back toward the wall around Land's End, climbed over and made her way surreptitiously back to the house.

She went up to her room, took a bath and changed into clean clothes. Cindy and Cassie were sitting quietly in the two armchairs facing each other across a small fire in the den. There was no sign of Thorn.

Cassie said as Jenny came in, "There's a cold supper for you in the kitchen." She got up.

Jenny knew she couldn't eat much, but she let Cassie go out to get it.

Cindy said, "I'm sorry, Jen. I didn't know."

Jenny thought that she would like no one to mention any of this. She wanted the whole summer to be forgotten. She didn't want to have to put into words what she was feeling. She looked out through the French windows to where the peach espaliers were spread across the wall of the kitchen garden to catch the hottest of the summer sun. Now, in the darkness, they looked like veins crawling up the wall. As she watched, she saw Thorn, a shadow in the night, come through the door in the garden wall and close it behind him. His shoulders were bent and he had the collar of his leather jacket turned up against the cool of the evening. Fall would be early this year: Already the nights were cold.

At the sight of Thorn, Jenny's heart had seemed to squeeze and the tears came back into her eyes. She couldn't look at Cindy. She felt like such a fool.

"It isn't your fault," she managed to say. She wondered how much Cassie had told Cindy of what had happened that summer. She wondered if Cindy knew that Jenny had fallen in love with Thorn, fallen in love with the way he had made a joke of everything, of the way he was so strong and brave, of the way he was alone in the world and not bitter or complaining. Fallen in love, she now realized, with a lie, a long string of lies.

Cassie came back with her dinner on a tray. Cassie said with a false brightness, "I think we're going to have to bag the peaches this year. There could be an early frost."

Jenny tried to eat the cold cuts and salad that Cassie had prepared. She knew she was being a baby, a little child sulking and she knew how Cassie felt about that; no matter how you felt, you never let your moods affect your guests. That was one of Cassie's rules. But it was as though her heart refused for the first time to listen to her mind and no matter how hard she tried, every time she tried to talk normally her thoughts wandered off into the memories of the summer with Thorn.

The whole summer had been a lie and she had fallen in love with the biggest lie of all. She had fallen in love with Thorn.

It was Cassie who suggested that they all go to bed early that night and no one objected.

On other summer visits Cindy and Jenny had sat up into the early hours of the morning talking and talking about what had happened since they parted and scheming and planning about the future, but though Cindy came into Jenny's room when she had changed into her robe, this time the conversation just kept dying. Finally Cindy had stretched and gone to her own room pretending to be tired.

Jenny had thought she'd lie awake but instead she dropped right off into a dreamless sleep. She slept undisturbed right through until eleven the next morning.

Cindy was at the beach when she came down.

Cassie, serving breakfast to Jenny, had one of her no-nonsense looks about her. She said, "Child, the hardest thing in life is to see the other person's point of view."

"He's afraid," Jenny said flatly.

"Maybe he thought the person he was raised to be was a fraud," Cassie said. "Maybe this is the person he wanted to be. Nothing's changed, Jenny. He's still Thorn."

But that was the greatest betrayal of all. Even Cassie didn't think she was right.

Jenny went down to the beach to spend the day with Cindy, but Cindy was having a good time. Jenny felt terrible because she was acting like a child, but she couldn't help it.

Thorn stayed out of the way. He stayed away from meals, and he worked hard by himself in the garden. Once she caught him standing on a dune in the distance watching her and Cindy, and she wanted to stand up and run to him but she couldn't. Her body had a mind of its own, and she couldn't get up. What's more, at the sight of him, two strong feelings seem to course through her. She longed to be with him again, and she hated him, hated him for letting her listen to all those lies and hated him for letting him fall in love with her.

And then on the third day Cindy had come down to breakfast and said, "Guess what, Daisy called and she wants me to join her in Paris. She's going to marry this yo-yo."

Both Jenny and Cassie had known that it was a lie. But they had gone along with it while Cindy packed and Cassie read the train schedules.

Now Cassie was driving them along the narrow beach front road by the lighthouse. "Do you want to eat?" Cassie asked her.

"Not really," Jenny said.

They got out of the car and walked along the beach until they were in the shadow of the lighthouse. They sat down and said nothing for a while.

Then Cassie said, "I could send him away."

Jenny didn't reply. Finally Jenny said, "The summer's almost gone anyway. The fete's next week. You'll need him for that."

Cassie accepted that. When she spoke at the end of some more minutes she said, "Try not to hate him. He feels as bad as you do."

But Jenny didn't want to hear about Thorn's feelings. She got up and walked back to the car.

Cassie came back and got in and they drove silently back to Land's End. As they came up the drive she saw Thorn mowing the front lawn for the next week's fete and her heart jumped two beats. He had his shirt off and the sunlight played on the muscles of his back. At the sound of the car, he turned and looked toward them. His face was drenched with sweat. He stood tall with one hand holding the old hand mower, and with his forearm, he wiped the sweat from his brow. His face was flat and emotionless.

"Pride can be a terrible price to pay," Cassie said as she turned off the ignition of the car.

For one second Jenny wanted to get out of the car and walk toward Thorn and put her arms about him and her head on his chest. She wanted to say nothing, just wait for his arms to come about her and hold onto her and feel safe the way she had felt a week ago and for all the weeks since he first kissed her on the dock. But before she could, the hurt flooded back through her. She got out of the car without a word or a glance at him and went into the cool shelter of Land's End.

10

Jenny heard the gulls cry with joy at the first light. She climbed out of her bed and drew back the old faded cotton striped curtains. Sunlight silvered the accordion crests of the ocean. The dunes were the palest shade of beige rolling along the shore.

A lone figure was walking at the water's edge, head down, hands in his pockets, and it was a few moments before Jenny realized with a shock that it was Thorn.

Her heart stopped at the recognition, hesitated, and then raced on as all the confused memories of his betrayal returned with force.

She turned away, letting the curtain drop so that her room was once again bathed in the soft shadows of dawn, and went about preparing for the day. She wanted to walk out of the house, go to the station and take the train into the city, but she couldn't disappoint Cassie. Cassie had looked forward all summer to this day. Land's End would be open to the public to host the hospital charity fete.

Already Jenny could hear the sounds of the workmen who had come to put the finishing touches to the tents and stalls. As she opened her bedroom door, she heard Cassie's long trill of laughter like a bird's, soaring with happiness and pleasure at the sheer joy of the day.

The floor at the foot of the long staircase had been washed and polished. The black and white marble squares shone with the brilliance of a chessboard. The French doors at the end of the hall stood open, the panes spotless and shining in the light of the rising sun. Through them Jenny had a glimpse of the back lawn, immaculate, a carpet of bright green grass, the result of all Thorn's rolling and watering, of his careful cutting and grooming under Jenny's watchful eye.

She had felt closer to Thorn than anyone in her life except Cassie, and now she knew she had never known him at all. He had invented himself, offered her a character out of a book or play and she had believed him, trusted him and given him back the truth.

She understood finally the meaning of that secret smile, the sly sideways look from under the thick lashes, brown eyes, focusing on her face as though there was no one else in the world but the two of them.

That, too, she supposed now, was a trick, an actor's trick, rehearsed, as he had written his own lines, invented his own part, holding back everything that was truly him.

A loud shout from the front of the house signalled the rising of the marquee. Jenny pushed all the troubling thoughts away and hurried down the last dozen stairs. Outside two dozen workmen struggled to pull the big red and white tent upright. Inch by inch it rose like a small candy striped mountain.

A pickup truck hauling a horse trailer turned off the roadway in the distance and began the long drive to the house. Two ponies, ears flat to their heads to catch the breeze, watched indifferently as the truck circled past the marquee tent to where the workmen were securing the rope supports. Then they drove off down toward the stables where the pony rides would be held in the show ring Thorn had restored.

Thorn, Thorn, Thorn, Jenny thought. A good name for him and the anger that came behind the pain drove her back into the house to get on with her own day. When Cassie found her she was pounding hamburger patties into small round shapes in preparation for supervising the snack bar.

"Darling," Cassie said, coming up behind her, "I think that meat is quite dead already."

Jenny looked at the row of hamburger patties she had lined up on the old kitchen counter. Each of them was as thin as a wafer and hammered flat. She had a pretty good idea whom she had been thinking of in her subconscious.

"I'm nervous," she said, laughing at the sight of all those ruined patties. "We served hundreds of people every week in the old days," Cassie said. "Land's End will survive."

"In the old days we had servants," Jenny reminded her.

"Well, today we have the whole local Junior League," Cassie said, "and the hospital committee. I wouldn't worry."

As though on cue the door to the hall opened and a flurry of print dresses announced the arrival of the hospital volunteers. Laughter and cries of excitement rang off the high ceiling and Cassie headed out in triumph at the center of a flock of women.

Jenny shaped the hamburgers into patties again, stacked them between wax paper ready for the grill that was being set up outside, and put them into the freezer. Other girls came into the kitchen now, laughing and giggling at the thought of the day ahead. Jenny went out through the house into the garden.

The garden had been transformed into a carnival of bright colors. A row of stalls stood along the edge of the drive, each with a tanned boy or girl behind it dressed in a striped shirt of blue, or yellow or pink, each wearing a straw hat. The noise level had risen to a low rumble of excitement that hummed through the early summer day like an electrical current. She saw Cassie in the distance setting up the flower stall. A blond head rose from among the knee high silver buckets of water for the cut flowers and Jenny caught her breath, but when the boy turned, it wasn't Thorn and another feeling, as annoying as the first went through her. This time it was disappointment, and that made her angry with herself.

She didn't want to miss Thorn.

She went off toward the walled kitchen garden where the barbeque stands were being set up safely out of the way of the tumbling children.

Here in the walled garden the noise of the first moments of the fete was muffled by the espaliered peach trees that grew neatly pruned against the wall, Thorn's efforts again. He was everywhere. She touched the rough, dark green leaves noticing how much more healthy they looked already this year. Next year there would be a fine crop of peaches. Sometimes trees, like people, just had to be left to rest.

Unconsciously she looked upward at the open windows of Thorn's room above the garage. The windows were open, the faded blue and white striped curtains gently moving in the breeze from the ocean.

Her assistants arrived then, a girl of thirteen and a boy of twelve. The girl took charge with all the authority of a general, and Jenny couldn't help smiling at the way she bossed the boy around, treating him as both her property and her servant. Cassie would have approved.

Jenny moved as in a dream, leaving the preparation of the paper plates and napkins, the cups, the straws, to the intense dark-haired little girl and her love-struck helper. "Poor you," Jenny thought as she watched the boy rushing about his duties and then she had to laugh at herself.

But then another thought came to her, something she had read, "There is always one who loves and one who is loved." She had no doubt who was the one who loved in this little pair. The boy could hardly take his eyes off the girl. He fled about the walled garden as though every command she spoke was a treasure, every order a gift.

"Do you believe that?" Jenny had asked Cassie when she first read it.

And Cassie, who believed in love the way she believed in miracles and happy endings, had thought, her eyes searching back through the past to her own great love, Cassie's grandfather. Jenny had been sure she had been going to say "No," but instead Cassie had said, "Love's never even, I think"—she had looked directly at Jenny—"but then you don't want it to be if you're really in love. You want to give as much as you can. You can't bargain in love. You just give because you can't help yourself and you wouldn't want to anyway. Love's like living in another country where there are other laws entirely."

That was a typical Cassie statement and Jenny had accepted it as such, for Cassie inhabited another world anyway where princesses lived in palaces by the sea and princes came to rescue them and even the hard times were only a chapter in a story on the way to a happy ending.

Real life wasn't like that.

The sun had risen higher in the sky. Beyond the garden wall music had begun, marches pumped from loudspeakers in the upper windows of the house. Later there would be a band and a dance floor on the lawn above the sea, but for the day, there was recorded music, trumpets and saxophones and drums like a country fair. Jenny caught the mood of the music, and she turned her face toward the sun, leaning her head back against the warm brick walls of the garden with her eyes closed.

"Not there, dummy!" the girl's voice said. "Over there!" Jenny smiled without opening her eyes.

"Where do you want this?" Thorn's voice said nearby and at first Jenny thought she had dreamt it. She opened her eyes to see him standing over her, the sun behind his head, his shoulders in the blue work shirt bunched with the pressure of the ice chest he was carrying.

Her voice wouldn't come at first. But when she found it, she said, "Over there in the shade." And though she was startled, she still could hear how similar her own tones were to the girl who had been bossing the boy around. The boy and girl stood quietly now to one side watching Thorn. Even they were struck dumb by his sheer good looks.

"Hi," he said to them as he went past lugging the ice chest. Neither of them could do more than just nod at him in worship.

Anger helped Jenny to get herself in control again. "That's fine," she said when he had placed the chest in the shade of the far wall where the ice would last longer.

Thorn stood tall then and looked at her, his hands hanging at his side. His shirt was stained with the effort of carrying the heavy chest. He was about to say something. She knew that look when his face went entirely blank, but before he could speak, she said, "We'll open the gates at noon exactly," and turned away, dismissing him but not before she saw despair clearly on his face. He turned abruptly on his heel and went out of the garden, letting the heavy wooden gate slam loudly behind him.

The girl and boy looked at her accusingly.

A man from the village came in then with a bag of charcoal, and the boy and girl forgot about Jenny. She knew that they thought she couldn't be a very nice person if she didn't get along with someone as fine as Thorn. Jenny shook her head at that thought. Appearances were everything, it seemed, no matter what teachers taught you. Cassie, too, for that matter. Cassie believed that it was what inside a person that counted, but she liked things dressed up anyway, the old house painted, the gardens planted and all of that took money.

Thorn had plenty of money. He had run away from it and come up here and played at being a gardener for a while.

She went inside the house while the man from the village lit the barbeque, and the boy and girl started to haul cases of Coke and ginger ale out from the kitchen to put on ice.

Without knowing why, she went upstairs and down the hall to Cassie's room. She had a strange premonition, a feeling that this was a turning point today for the house, for Cassie and for herself. Cassie's room was the way it always was. The big four-poster bed sat right in the center of the floor and about it was all that was left of the furniture that had once filled this vast mansion.

All that was left of the past, this huge quiet house and some pieces of cloth and furniture.

And memories, as Cassie would insist. No one can ever take your memories away.

Jenny had some memories that she wished would go.

She went to the window and stood in the shadow of the curtains looking down at the garden. The fete and the opening of Land's End to the public after all this time had brought the whole summer population.

Jenny saw Cassie down there, happy, as she took another dollar for the hospital fund from a father who bent to help his son steady his arm as he threw a ball at a row of bottles set up in the back of Cassie's booth.

And then she saw Thorn again unexpectedly as he lifted a little boy onto the back of a pony. The child turned to Thorn trustingly. Thorn smiled at him with that slow, secret smile that struck at Jenny even at this distance so that everyone else in between, the crowds, seemed to fade and for one second there was just the two of them in the world, Thorn and herself, as there had been in so many moments through the summer.

The curtain fell from her hand, and the room floated in an underwater light filtered through the rose silk. The summer would be over soon and she would leave here and go back to college.

And Thorn would go.

He'd tire of this game of being poor and go home.

The sun was directly above the Chinese pavilion roof of the boathouse and suddenly she realized with a shock, that meant it was noon and time for the kitchen garden to open to hamburgers and hot dogs, soft drinks and potato chips. She raced out of Cassie's bedroom, all thought of the last months gone, and took the hall at a run, down the winding staircase two steps at a time and out through the kitchen.

The boy and girl had done a good job, everything was ready and the barbeque was glowing, with the man from the village beaming happily.

"Ready, Miss Castle," he said. "Shall we let them in?"

Jenny grabbed her apron from where it was hung on the peach tree, tied it quickly around her and laughed. "All right," she cried. "Let in the starving masses!" and the boy ran to the gate. All four of the workers, Jenny, the village man and the boy and girl, however, were struck dumb by the sight outside. A mob of people were all lined up ready for lunch.

From that moment on, Jenny didn't have time for

another thought as she dropped hamburgers on the griddle, hot dogs, slathered buns with mayonnaise and worked on through the afternoon feeding what seemed to be an endless line of starving people. The girl sat near the cash box counting the money in and the change out and the boy opened soda bottles while the village man stocked the barbeque and ran for ice as they needed it.

The crowd dwindled toward late afternoon and Jenny realized that she had quite forgotten her earlier thoughts in all the hustle of the hours of work. Cassie came bustling into the garden, her eyes aglow. "We've made two hundred dollars at the stall," she said, laughing like a little girl who had sold her first glass of lemonade from a roadside stall. "Can you believe it? The committee says this is the most successful fete they've ever had. The hospital will have a mint to spend this winter. Isn't that wonderful?"

Jenny hugged Cassie. "Yes," she said, "and it was your idea."

"And . . ." Cassie said automatically but stopped. Jenny knew what Cassie had been about to say. She had been about to say, "And Thorn's."

Jenny found that she wasn't as hurt or worried as she had been earlier. The hard day's work had drained a lot of her anger. But she still didn't want to talk about him or hear his name. Instead she said, "What's it like out there?" gesturing beyond the garden wall to the place where the rest of the fete had been held.

"Quieter," Cassie said. "People are going home to change. The clean-up crew arrived from the beach club to get the garden ready for the dance." The juniors of the beach club had volunteered to clean the grounds after the day's crowd while the workmen from the hospital erected the dance floor on the lawn over the sea.

Just then a crew came into the garden carrying plastic bags with the afternoon's trash. The boy and girl who had helped all day came over to say they were going home to change and went out hand in hand.

Cassie sighed again at the sight of them. "So young," she said.

Jenny said, "You are an incurable romantic, Cassie." She put her arm about her shoulder to lead her inside. "Would you like to rest before the evening?"

"Rest," Cassie said. "Of course, I can't rest. You're treating me like an old person!"

"Well, I'm going to soak in a hot tub and rest," Jenny said. "I'm going to drop in my tracks before the night is out if I don't rest."

"You youngsters have no stamina," Cassie said. "If your grandfather were here he'd be building the dance floor himself right at this moment, and then he'd go right on and dance all night."

Jenny went wearily up the staircase to her bedroom. From the window over the lane, she saw that the workmen had staked out a huge square and were in the process of placing planks across the supporting boards. Beyond them the lawn sloped down to

105

the dunes, gilded chrome in the last rays of the setting sun and the sea, stretching away to the horizon on a bright metallic plain ripped with waves. A single sailboat bent keeled homeward before the wind, sails silhouetted against the pale blue sky and already the round wafer of the full moon could be seen in the sky.

She lay down on her bed in her clothes thinking that she would rest just for a moment and then get up and take a bath to revive her. But she dropped right away into a deep sleep where Land's End was as new and polished as it had been when her grandfather lived here, with music and guests everywhere, and gardens blooming with flowers and the drive filled with carriages, where a mahogany sailboat with a bright red sail limned the horizon over a deep blue sea, where music played and over it all a full moon floated, and as the clouds passed in front of the moon, they made shadows that made it almost look as though the moon were smiling, her fair, dark-eyed lips parted in a smile full of secrets.

11

She woke with a start to find her room in pitch darkness. Soft music drifted up from the lawn below the house. Getting out of bed, she lifted the curtain and looked down at the garden. The dance floor was in place, poles at each corner and between them strings of small white lights. Off to the side stood another tent, smaller than the marquee that had been put up earlier. This tent was black and white, lit with the same small star lights. Jenny could see waiters in white jackets moving behind a buffet set up behind a table draped in a long white linen cloth. The music came from a small, round bandstand in the corner of the terrace, and everywhere she looked there were flowers, stands of them in tall urns, roses and peonies, hollyhocks and dahlias, trailing vines of summer roses, and honeysuckles.

Jenny sighed. Cassie had her house the way it used to be. The first of the guests arrived, a small group of summer visitors, identifiable by their bright evening clothes, the two women trailing clouds of chiffon behind them, the men in light blazers. Cassie would have her night after all, one last night when Land's End was the way it used to be.

Jenny dropped the curtain again and went into the bathroom. Her spirits lifted as she heard the first strains of a waltz, the violins catching the mood of the summer night. She ran the old four-legged tub to the brim with hot water, dropped in a handful of rose bath salts and stepped in.

"Jenny?"

"I'm in the tub, Cassie."

Cassie knocked gently on the bathroom door and opened it a crack. Jenny slid under the cloud of bubbles. "Darling?" Cassie said.

"Come in, Cassie."

Cassie shyly pushed open the door and Jenny felt a smile begin slowly. A smile of such happiness that even wet she wanted to get right out of the tub and hug her grandmother. Cassie was beautiful. Dressed in a dress she had saved all these years, the deep blue Chinese silk shimmering as she moved, gold shoes kept in tissue paper for twenty years peeking out from beneath the hem, a cameo on a blue velvet ribbon at her neck and her hair pulled back and pinned with two tortoiseshell combs brought back by her father from some long ago journey.

"Oh, Cassie, you're beautiful," Jenny said.

"Just like the old days," Cassie said shyly.

"Just like the old days," Jenny said, and she felt tears come to her eyes at the sight of her grandmother, tiny and old, but beautiful, dressed up for Land's End's last party.

Neither of them knew what to say then. Finally Jenny said quietly, "You should go down to greet your guests, Cassie."

The steam rising from the tub made it hard for Jenny to know if what she saw was true, but she thought Cassie's eyes were glittering also. Cassie said, "I love you, darling."

"And I love you, Cassie," Jenny said, "and if you don't watch out, I'm going to get right out of this tub and hug you soaking wet."

Cassie smiled and closed the bathroom door. The water had cooled. Jenny reached a practiced foot down the tub and turned the large brass handle with her toes, filling the tub with more warm water, the feeling of well-being flooding through her. The band had switched to a foxtrot, the faster beat muffled by the walls of the old house that seemed to hum with a happiness of its own.

Jenny dried herself carefully on a thick towel, shook her hair free and went into her bedroom. From her window she could see the strings of lights that edged the gardens. The guests moved, light bright noctural flowers in the summer night.

The summer was coming to an end. Looking at herself in the mirror, she tried to see if there was any change in her. She saw a girl with clear eyes, fair hair that fell to her shoulders, a slim athletic body. She had grown up, she knew. Her childhood was behind her. And her first love.

She went to her closet and chose a cornflower blue dress with slim straps. She put it on and tied up her hair with a ribbon to match. As she reached behind her head to tie the ribbon, she remembered that Thorn had bought it for her at a market fair where they had gone to deliver the vegetables. The ribbon was pure silk and matched the color of her eyes exactly, making them shine like sapphires, as Thorn had said when he tied it about her head that day.

Jenny sighed. Somewhere in the last hours her anger at him had gone. She hadn't forgiven him, but she didn't hate him either.

She stepped into high-heeled sandals and stood back. She was beautiful.

She went out of her bedroom and down into the main hall. Cassie was beaming in the distance at the sight of her home filled with people and, indeed, Land's End did look splendid, shining as it used to when Cassie was young.

Jenny went out onto the terrace and stood there looking at the dancers. The band was sitting in three rows playing the old tunes that Cassie loved and the dancers swirled in circles around and around on the raised dance floor.

She knew without turning that Thorn was behind her. Her heart was steady, but she waited, and when he put his hand on her shoulder, she allowed herself to be turned slowly until she was facing him. He looked sad. The planes beneath his eyes had dark circles from sleepless nights.

He didn't say he was sorry. He said, "Will you dance with me?"

She nodded and together they went hand in hand down the steps that they had weeded together and across the lawn to the dance floor.

The music changed as they stepped onto the dance floor and Thorn put his strong arm about her and drew her gently to him as the music started again. They danced the first dance together without a word and then the next. The music changed again to something faster and Thorn took her hand and led her off the dance floor. They walked out of the light to where the dunes sloped away from the lawn and he stood facing her.

"I'll say it if you want me to," he said.

"No," she said.

"I didn't mean it," he said. "I just wanted to be somebody new. I just wanted people to like me for myself and not because my family was rich. I wanted people to respect me and I made you hate me."

"I don't hate you, Thorn," Jenny said.

Thorn sighed. "I'm going home tomorrow," he said.

Jenny wanted to say, "Please stay, Thorn. We'll find a way."

Somewhere in her heart she would always love

Thorn because he had been her first love, but this was real life and not a fairy tale. Thorn had to go home to Palm Beach, and Jenny had to go to college.

Jenny stood on her tiptoes to kiss his cheek. "Good luck, Thorn, whoever you are," she said, and turning, she walked back alone toward the music and the lights.

Epilogue

Snowflakes fell softly past the dormitory window as Jenny stood looking out at the unbroken plain of white that stretched way into the night. She held Cindy's letter in her hand.

Cindy had decided not to go to college that year. She might go back to school the following one. Her plans had suddenly become uncertain at the end of last summer after she left Land's End. She had gone first to see her father again and then south to Palm Beach to see Daisy.

". . . Daisy needs me," Cindy had written. "I think she finally sees that she may end her life alone and she's scared, though she is too proud to admit it. She's gone from one husband to the next, looking for the perfect man and I think now she's beginning to see that *nobody's* perfect."

There was a new maturity in Cindy's letters, and though Jenny knew that was good, she felt a small loss, as though somehow by Cindy's growing up, she was losing her best friend.

Two bright lights pierced the curtain of snow where the highway lined the campus near the distant foothills. If the snow kept falling like this the roads would be closed by morning. The snowplows were already out. Jenny wondered if she'd make her flight tomorrow to join Cassie. Land's End had been sold. Cassie had found a nice apartment in the town near the beach and seemed very happy discovering the mysteries of dishwashers and reliable hot water heaters and rooms that didn't have drafts blowing through them all winter.

The snowplow pushed its way steadily across the horizon. Voices outside Jenny's door burst into the verse of "Rudolph the Rednose Reindeer," then exploded into laughter as they disappeared down the hall.

Jenny looked at Cindy's letter again. Even Cindy's large sprawling handwriting had become neater. ". . . I don't know how to write this," Cindy wrote next, "or even whether I should. But I saw Thorn in Palm Beach. He'd lost weight and he didn't look happy. He asked about you, but I said I hadn't heard because I knew you wouldn't want me to give out any information." Here there was a wide gap in the letter as though Cindy had put down her pen for a while and come back to the letter later. "Anyway," she wrote when she took up the pen again, "he's disappeared again. He worked for his father for a while but they didn't get along. Thorn's just too independent, I guess, and he likes to do things his own way. I asked around and heard that he went down to the Keys for a while to work on a shrimper and then he threw up that job. He told someone that he was going north. He said there was someone he had to see and that's all I know, but I thought I'd better write and tell you because I have a pretty fair idea of where he's headed."

After that Cindy had added some inconsequential gossip about life among the very rich, then she ended the letter. "Much love, Cindy."

Jenny folded the letter carefully. The envelope lay among her books on the desk. Her suitcases were packed for tomorrow's flight home for Christmas. She walked over to the desk and picked up the envelope and carefully replaced the letter.

Carolling had begun in earnest downstairs in the hall—"Silent night, holy night . . ." The snow falling outside and the darkness and the sound of the voices from below brought tears to Jenny's eyes. She sighed, looked at the letter, then out again at the snow still falling heavily. The lights of the snowplow were pushing closer. "Please," she whispered her prayer to the night, "let the roads be open tomorrow. Please let the flight take off."

She had to get home. She had to. She had an important appointment she couldn't miss.

CINDY

1

Cindy was pondering the mysteries of life. Why, she wondered, were all pool attendants blond? Was there some sort of rule, or were brunettes simply smart enough not to apply? The blond in question perched on his high chair above the Palm Beach Country Club pool, moved his perfect head right at that moment and stared directly at her as though he could read her thoughts. Cindy felt the blush begin at her toes and rise through her legs and body until her face was burning as bright as the sun above Palm Beach.

She rolled over on her stomach on the lounge and stared into the depths of the pool. A very thin woman in a black tank suit was swimming lengths of the pool underwater, dark hair streaming out behind her. Cindy watched her do two lengths without surfacing for air. I am surrounded by exhibitionists, she decided, watching the woman submerge again after a perfect turn in which she surfaced, rolled to the end of the pool, took air and started right in on more lengths. Everyone here is the thinnest, the blondest, the richest. What was she, she wondered, scrutinizing the pool from behind oversized dark glasses. I am either the youngest or the oldest, she decided rolling over with a sigh and sitting up. All the other girls her age had gone off to college except for the imminent nervous breakdowns, Ronnie Webster and Susan Lockwood, who were being kept close to home so someone could keep an eye on them. Ronnie, at sixteen, was competing for the most drunk driving tickets on the Florida coast and Susan, it was rumored, had had a bad romance but Cindy, try as she did, couldn't get any decent news on that.

It seemed to Cindy, looking at her half-written letter on the pool table, that the least a girl owed her friends if she had a bad romance was all the details.

The blond attendant had gone back to watching the children in the shallow end of the pool. Why was she wasting her time even thinking about pool attendants, Cindy wondered: The rules were firm. No guests were allowed to go out with or even have a meal off the grounds with any of the people who worked here.

Daisy had broken that rule once, Cindy knew.

120

Daisy had dated a tennis pro for one season but even Daisy, who was a natural victim and had to witness every accident, couldn't just be told about it, had dropped her tennis pro when the Christmas mail started coming in and it was all cards, no invitations.

Ve haf our vays, Cindy thought, in a mock German accent. The old social dragons who ran Palm Beach knew how to enforce their rules.

She picked up her letter to Jenny. Should she tell her about Thorn? Cindy had seen him once at a Junior League dance in September, looking angry and ill at ease in his white dinner jacket, the summer tan from working outside, a deeper tan somehow than all these pool tans, still dark on his face. His hair was cut shorter than he'd worn it when she last saw him, and she thought that was probably his father's influence. She had heard Thorn was working with his father, learning to take over the thousands of acres of orange groves that the family owned. But she had also heard that he wasn't getting along with his father either. The two of them were too much alike. They both wanted to do things their way.

She took up her pen. "There's something I don't know whether I should tell you . . ." she began.

She finished her letter, sealed it and gathered up her belongings. The blond in the big chair watched her leave with the look of a disapproving god. Cindy was sure he saw every tiny ripple of extra weight that Daisy was so adamant she lose.

She changed in her cabana, left the letter at the

desk to be mailed and went out to the car Daisy had bribed her with to stay the season instead of going to school.

Cindy would have stayed anyway. She had a lot to think about on her own, and the look she saw in Daisy's eyes these days, a sort of far-off fear, had her concerned, but when Daisy called her out of the house after breakfast one morning and there in the driveway was a shining silver Mercedes, Cindy had to admit her heart had rolled over once.

"Cindy, you're shallow," she lectured herself quite contentedly as she got in behind the wheel, adjusted her glasses on her face and tied back her hair with a silk scarf. She liked the effect she saw in the mirror. "Now," she thought, "if I could just contrive to spend every public hour behind the wheel of this car and never have to stand up or walk across a room, I could be stunning."

Short of being crippled, there seemed no prospect of that, so she put the car in gear and headed off to meet Daisy at the health club.

She drove down the coast thinking about Jenny off in the Midwest at college. Jenny had always known what she wanted: she wanted to grow up and be normal and have a nice simple life. Land's End for Jenny had just been a big house where her grandmother lived. Now that they had both graduated, Cindy thought they probably wouldn't see much of each other and that made her sad. Jenny had been Cindy's best friend for as long as she could remember, but the time came when people grew up and went their own ways.

You had to be careful, too, Cindy was thinking as she turned in at the parking lot of the health spa, where you headed on your journey. There was Daisy's Rolls Royce convertible, beige and tan, parked off to the side. Daisy's journey had taken her here eventually three times a week for relentless workouts, trying to stay young.

Cindy pulled up to the door. She left the motor running and reached back for her gym clothes. When she turned around she was looking directly into two of the deepest brown eyes she had ever seen. Startled, she moved back slightly but then the car jockey opened her door and she got a better look at him: he was like a miniature statue, five eight or nine, with jet black hair, a muscled body, every inch of which could be seen through his white tennis shirt and slim hips in clean blue jeans. His sneakers were so white they shone. "Hi," he said flashing a smile as bright as his sneakers.

When Cindy got out of the car, she saw that he was tall. He stood a head above her. He was perfect in every way, as far as she could see.

"Your Mom's here," he told her.

Cindy laughed and the bright smile disappeared. "I'm sorry," she said, "I was thinking what Daisy would say if she heard you call her *Mom.*"

The boy was blushing under his tan. "I'm sorry," he muttered, looking down at his feet and trying to get around Cindy without looking into her eyes. "Mrs. Marlow is here."

"Mrs. Halston," Cindy said. "Mrs. Marlow was two years ago."

The anger that flashed through his eyes caught Cindy by surprise. She had thought she was making a joke. Daisy hadn't been Mrs. Marlow for four years. And she'd only briefly been Mrs. Halston. She was between engagements, so to speak, which was part of the reason for all this working out at spas. "I got the name off her car keys," the boy said sullenly. "She told me to look out for you."

Cindy felt stupid. The Rolls Royce had been a gift from Jake Marlow. It would be like Daisy to leave that name on the key ring. She wouldn't think to look at the name under the leather tag and she only used the car when she was down here. But it was the *Mom* that Daisy had been laughing at. Daisy didn't allow Cindy to call her *Mother* anymore, let alone *Mom.*

"I didn't mean to be rude," she said trying to apologize, but the boy was behind the wheel of her car. He put it in gear and drove off without a word.

"Might as well start on my feet," she thought as she trudged into the spa. "If I can get them smaller, maybe I can get both in my mouth at the same time."

She signed in and went into the ladies' locker room. "We spend most of our days dressing and undressing," she thought as she got out of her clothes and wrapped herself in the towel the woman attendant brought her. "Your mother is in the steam room," the woman told her.

"Thank you," Cindy said, and wrapped up like some Halloween ghost, dragged her long towel out, down the hall to the steam room. In there all she could see were prostrate forms wrapped like mummies lying on shelves amid the humid air. "Daisy?" she called softly.

"Mmmmmm," was the reply from a body on the corner rack.

Cindy dragged over there. Daisy lay as though prepared for the last rites, the towel beneath her perfect body stretched to its fullest. But her face seemed to have changed color and gone bright green.

"Hi," Cindy said, taking off her own towel and laying it on a nearby rack.

"Mmmmmm," said Daisy.

"What?" asked Cindy louder, throwing herself down on the towel. Could being thin be worth this? she wondered. Were there no boys left in the world who wanted a "handful of woman?" she thought, using a phrase she had heard once in a John Wayne movie that struck her as a really sensible way to look at women.

"I'm wearing a vegetable peel," Daisy shouted, so loud Cindy sat straight up. "Oh, God," Daisy said, "I think I cracked it." She wrapped her towel about her and hurried out of the steam.

"I will just die right here," Cindy decided, lying back down again. "I am surrounded by lunatics. All my life I have been surrounded by lunatics. All the years ahead I will be surrounded by lunatics." The image of Cassie's face at Land's End floated through her mind. Cassie was a lunatic, too, she guessed, but somehow Cassie's lunacy took a more sensible form. Cassie hired strangers off the street as her gardeners who turned out to be heir to half of Florida, but Cassie didn't spend half her day exercising, being pounded into shape, wrapped in a vegetable peel, massaged with mysterious oils, draped in clothes cut so stunningly to disguise the imperfections of aging figures that the designers should be charged under the Truth-in-Advertising laws for crass deceit, all so that they could appear for a few starlit hours among people whom they had known all their lives and who had gone through exactly the same thing that day.

Among Cindy's new rules for living that she was compiling secretly was the suggestion that all the people in Palm Beach throw their keys in a hat on New Year's Eve and just pull them out at midnight like a lottery. Whomever you were matched up with, you went to live with for one year. That would save a fortune in divorce lawyers and achieve about the same thing.

When she thought she was about ready to slip off the rack, she was wet with sweat. She wrapped herself up again and went out to plunge herself into an icy shower.

Daisy was being pounded by a thick-armed masseuse when she caught up with her in the massage room. From the sounds coming out of Daisy, the woman was killing her. Cindy waved the tips of her fingers at her mother and lay down on the next table. "The coward's massage," she told the thin, wiry woman who came up to her, "please."

She lay there having her body stretched and pounded, listening to her mother's wails of pain and the thought came as clear as a telegram, *This is the last time I am going to do this. This is dumb.*

But she knew this wasn't the place to have that discussion. For all she knew Daisy might be smeared in some mysterious oil brought over from Egypt by priests of Cleopatra that would turn rancid at the first sour word.

The masseuse finished with Daisy who lay there muttering under her breath words that sounded from where Cindy lay suspiciously like curses. Finally she allowed herself to be helped up and stumbled out of the room.

Cindy waited a couple of minutes more and said, "That's enough, thank you."

The wiry woman held onto her arm. "You're not finished yet," she said in a voice that would, anywhere else in the world have been taken for a threat.

"Oh, yes, I am," Cindy said, getting up. She smiled so that the masseuse would know she held her no ill will for bodily assault and trailed out after Daisy. She found her being made up in the main salon. She was a remarkable looking woman for her age, whatever that was, Cindy thought. Her hair was still thick and fair, her skin like a peach, but around the eyes there were tiny wrinkles that no amount of makeup could hide and at the corners of her mouth there were the slightest signs of drooping as though finally the face wanted to tell the truth about the character inside. Daisy was never entirely pleased with anything, as Cindy knew, which was part of her endless search for Mr. Right, but no one else knew that unless they were either related to her by birth or marriage.

Daisy caught Cindy looking at the lines in her face. "I'm thinking of flying up to New York for a few days," she said, as the makeup man stepped back. Daisy was beautiful, Cindy admitted. In her own way she was courageous. She wouldn't give in to the years no matter how much effort it cost.

Cindy had a pretty good idea why Daisy was flying north. She'd been on the phone for weeks getting the name of the best plastic surgeon to correct the lines about her eyes.

"Do you want to come?" Daisy seemed a lot more solemn lately. Part of that was because if she smiled, the lines deepened. But some of it was because she seemed to be thinking her own thoughts a lot.

Cindy wanted to reach down and hug her mother and say, "Forget it! Mom, let's eat pasta for a week instead and lie in the sun without sunscreens." But she knew that would be as confusing to Daisy as if she had said, "Let's shop at Sears this season and save some dough."

"Do you want me to come?" Cindy asked, meaning, *do you need me?*

"I'll be gone about four days," Daisy said, giving

Cindy the clue that this was one consultation she wanted to go through alone.

"I'll be okay," Cindy said.

Daisy got out of the chair and allowed herself to be unwrapped from the mauve robe that protected her dress. She was wearing a simple linen dress with sleeves. The skin under her arms was beginning to sag ever so slightly. "I'm having lunch with Marge and Harriet at the Patio. Do you want to join us?"

"No," Cindy said, "you go ahead. I'll meet you at home later."

She kissed her mother and watched her leave the salon. "A lovely woman," the attendant said, stepping back for Cindy to get into the chair.

Cindy looked at the chair. She looked at the day outside just visible through the thin horizontal windows at the top of the walls. The sun was shining in a bright blue sky. "Not today, thank you," she said.

She hurried through the spa to the front door. A new parking attendant came to ask her which car she wanted. The other attendant brought around the silver Mercedes and she tipped him.

She put the car in gear and started down the lanes of cars of the shopping center. She saw him as she slowed to move into traffic along the coast highway. He was waiting to cross the highway toward a fast food stand. She tooted lightly on her horn and he turned quickly as though he might know her, but then he saw the car and his smile faded. He came back without any expression on his face, and Cindy knew he thought he was being summoned by one of the rich and that he had to come because he needed the job at the spa.

"Can I help you?" he asked, still without any expression except deep in his dark brown eyes, where Cindy saw emotions moving like tides.

"You want to go for a Big Mac?" she asked.

He looked startled for a moment, then he laughed. "Sure," he said.

He didn't seem to know what to do after that. He just stood there. "Well, get in, dummy," Cindy said. He put one hand on the door and leapt over it like she'd seen done in television movies and was sure he had too.

She pulled out into traffic heading for the golden arches visible in the distance. "With french fries," she said.

"What?" he said, but he was smiling as though he had heard.

"And a milk shake," Cindy said defiantly.

The boy leaned his head back on the seat smiling.

"They'll probably drum me out of the club if they ever hear," Cindy said.

"I'll never tell," the boy said.

"Promise?" Cindy asked, pulling the car into line behind a small compact at the hamburger stand.

"My word is my bond," the boy said holding out his hand.

Cindy shook it. She liked the feeling of his dry, firm handshake. "I'm Cindy," she said.

"Raul," the boy said. By the way he looked at her, Cindy thought that maybe she wouldn't have the milk shake after all, and a moment after perhaps a small fries would do. But no matter how wise it might be to try to keep some of the weight off, she wasn't going to give up the Big Mac. There were some things that were too great a sacrifice even for love.

2

Cindy heard the ringing of the telephone through the vast, wide halls of the house. She had to say one thing for Daisy, she could fill a house with her presence. Daisy had only been gone two days and already the house seemed more silent, more empty than Cindy could remember it ever having been.

She saw a maid hurrying down the polished tiled hall toward the telephone in the front hall. "I'll get it," Cindy called.

The young maid with long dark hair looked as startled as though Cindy had said she'd scrub the floor but she went off again with her dust mop and let Cindy pick up the telephone. The truth was Cindy was beginning to feel abandoned. She didn't know what she hated most, the feeling of loneliness that she felt creeping over her as silence was taking the house or the realization of just how much she missed Daisy. Daisy was life. "Hello," Cindy said into the receiver.

"Uh, uh . . ."

For one breathless moment Cindy thought she'd locked into a heavy breather. She'd heard about them. One of the girls at school had actually got three calls right in a row, spaced two weeks apart on last summer's vacation. She hadn't told anyone, but then the jerk of a caller had gotten her mother and he'd barely started to tell her his plans when she launched right in with a stern lecture that sent him packing.

But then the caller cleared his throat and said, "Is Cindy there?"

"Yup," Cindy said, "who's this?"

"Uh, uh . . . Raul."

She remembered him instantly, of course. How could she not. He was the only interesting person she'd met down here in three months. But she hadn't been back to the spa since Daisy flew north wrapped in scarves as though she was going into a cloister instead of just to see a noted surgeon who could take a tuck here and there and give her back her youth, or a good ten years of it anyway. Daisy had a sense of drama. By the time Cindy got back to the house she was already way into her new role, packing like a fury and chain smoking Parliament Lights as though the Pope had called and needed her advice within the day.

"Hi," Cindy said.

133

Raul didn't seem to get the picture. He let another long pause go by before he said, "Cindy?"

"In the flesh," Cindy said, noticing in the mirror over the hall table that the Big Mac she'd had with Raul seemed to have gone straight to her chin. Life was unfair all right. There was Jenny off in some lost colony in the Midwest where she could use this flesh to keep warm through the winter, and she was willing to bet she hadn't gained one ounce.

Another pause. This was getting awkward. "Hey, Raul," Cindy said, taking the bit between the teeth. "You want to come over here for dinner?"

"There?" The way he said it, you'd think she invited him to risk his life.

"Yeah, here," Cindy said.

This pause was not as long, but this was one strong young man. He wasn't to be tempted. "I was going to ask you to a movie," he said.

Cindy took all of a second and a half to think that over. "All right," she said. "When?"

"Tonight?" he ventured.

Well, he had backbone, she thought. She knew what he wanted and went after it. "Fine," she said, "what time?"

Another of his pauses. But before he spoke, she had a flash of insight. "You want me to pick you up?" she asked quickly. "I have to be downtown later in the afternoon."

She could hear the relief in his voice. "I thought we could maybe meet at the show," he said.

Cindy took down the directions and hung up. That

had to have taken guts, she thought, and a small warm sense of satisfaction crept through her. She'd had a good time with Raul at the burger joint. They'd bought their lunches and taken them back to the car and sat eating them in the sun with the top down, but she hadn't really expected him to call. She figured the spa had the same rules that the beach club did and he probably was breaking all sorts of regulations by having lunch with her.

But she'd liked him. He made her laugh. He had a quick smile and a happiness in his eyes, as though every moment was somehow something special itself, that she didn't see much among the people she'd been hanging out with since the fall. Still, when she'd asked him if she could drop him back at the spa, the smile had faded and he got out of the car, saying he'd hitch back up the highway.

She was glad she'd remembered that he'd hitched back to the spa. He didn't have a car, she realized. She couldn't think of anyone among her own acquaintances who didn't have cars or easy access to them.

Well, she thought with satisfaction as she went back through the house toward the garden, *the plot thickens*.

In the garden she watched a pair of butterflies chase each other in a demented fury around a hibiscus blossom and thought that she had no problem at all in accepting the fact that man had risen with the other animals from the same gooey mess of swamp. Here a minute ago she had been moping around this huge house that Daisy had wrestled as part of her spoils from a divorce lost back in the mists of time, and ten minutes later, with a date in the offing for the evening, there was a song in her heart. She knew exactly how the female butterfly felt, whichever of the two creatures she was. Cindy took a few extravagant leaps into the air with her arms flung wide with imaginary shawls and would have danced on past the neat row of gardenia bushes toward the bottom of the garden if she hadn't caught sight of one of the gardeners seemingly struck dumb by the sight. *Some people*, she reflected, *had no appreciation of culture*, as she slunk back into the house, her face flaming with embarrassment.

She went up to the two rooms, the bedroom and small sitting room, that her mother had designated as Cindy's this season and opened her closet. Two rooms was an ominous gift. Most vacations, she'd had one large room to herself because her mother had an unbroken stream of visitors through the winter. But this year she'd been given *two* rooms and when Daisy had suggested that a season spent together in Palm Beach might be a good idea for Cindy, Cindy had had an uneasy feeling that she was starting in on the first months of a life sentence as constant companion. She'd seen it happen: aging women with fading daughters trailing along behind them.

Well, it wasn't going to happen to Cindy, no matter how much she loved her mother. Not when there were Rauls around, Cindy thought, looking at her reflection smugly in the long mirror. She might not be Daisy, and it *could* be said, if you were a vicious, unprincipled person, that Cindy still carried a few extra pounds on her despite three months of following along behind Daisy to spas, but there was good blood there, no doubt about it. She had great hair, thick and springy, even if it did react to the Florida humidity as though someone had stuck her finger in an electric socket, and her face, though broad, was definitely pretty. She had a figure too— that was one thing a few extra pounds gave you, shape, and shape could be *molded*. Levi's were definitely out, no matter how much she longed to wear them. Levi's were a curse thought up by some evil magician in San Francisco to make opulent women cringe with fear. No, a simple skirt and blouse would do, she thought.

Then she had another thought. Raul had to be Latin. More than fifty percent of South Florida was now Spanish speaking. All the street signs were in both languages. And it was a well-known fact that Latin men liked their women discreet.

Discretion had never been Cindy's strong suit. She tended to speak right up with whatever was on her mind but in dress at least she could meet the challenge. She found a blue linen skirt and a blouse just a shade lighter than the skirt that made her red hair and bright green eyes do something special of their own.

She put the skirt and blouse on the bed and checked the time. Raul had suggested the eight o'clock show. It was just three o'clock. How was she going to fill in five hours?

Daisy always took a nap. Well, Daisy's naps were more like full-blown sleeps, particularly before a heavy date, but then Daisy was seldom just going to a movie in North Miami Beach. Daisy was usually planning a major safari after one of America's foremost industrialists and that took cunning and an unwavering eye, when you considered the competition for America's foremost industrialists.

Still Daisy had gotten more than her fair share of that particular big game, so she must know what she was doing. Cindy moved the blouse and skirt off the bed and kicked off her sandals. She lay down, closed her eyes and concentrated on sleep. But the house that half an hour ago had had all the gaiety of Grant's Tomb now suddenly was alive with sound. A vacuum cleaner hummed down the hall, the gardeners below took this moment to discuss fertilizer and for some reason that had to be personally directed against Cindy's happiness by some malicious higher power, the traffic out on the boulevard was louder than she'd ever heard it.

She opened her eyes and stared at the ceiling. That absorbed her for two of the longest minutes of her life before she swung her feet off the bed and sat there looking at her reflection in the long mirror of her closet door.

"You are only going on a date," she told herself. But of course Cindy knew without having to spell it out for herself that this was more than a date. Why was that? she asked. Because the butterflies that she already felt in her stomach were dancing every bit as dementedly as though around the hibiscus blossom down in the garden. It wasn't as though this was the first date she'd ever been on. She'd been to dances for as long as she had been able to stand up: dances for the graduation of nursery school where the nurses came along with the children, dances for the first few grades where she and Jenny had just stood in the corner and giggled while they stuffed their faces with cake, dances later on during the summer out at the beach club near Land's End when they had observed with awe the awful process whereby the girls were growing faster than the boys. "Like hugging teddy bears to you," Cindy had said one particularly terrible night when she and Jenny had towered over all the boys in the room as though they had taken some pill, like Alice in Wonderland, and just grown overnight. And even dances down here this winter.

She knew what it was, she realized suddenly. At all of those dances, she had been paired off with boys she'd known all her life.

Raul was a civilian. Raul came from the outside world. Raul was a real person. Fear ran through her. I will just absolutely gross him out with my attitudes and *I won't even know it!*

She had a very real sense that she would like to throw up, which didn't seem the right reaction to a date with a good-looking boy she'd had fun with over a hamburger two days before.

Well, she thought, if you stretched the truth, it wasn't really their *first* date anyway. Lunch had been their first date. If you allowed that, then this was their *second* date, and if he asked her out again, you might even be able to say they were going steady. By the time Daisy got back, she'd be engaged, and Daisy could spend the rest of the winter planning a large wedding.

Cindy pushed the thought of Daisy out of her mind.

But she had to admit that she had liked that thought of a *third* date with Raul. She now would have to play her cards absolutely right tonight, she saw. She thought of calling Jenny at college for advice but checking the time she saw that Jenny would be in class probably, and even if she did call, there would be so much explanation, and though Jenny had always stood by her, no matter what, no matter how, she thought that Jenny might not consider this as great a crisis as Cindy did, and might resent being called from nuclear physics or something where she was just about to split an atom to talk over Cindy's date with Raul.

She decided to go back to the beach club and swim a hundred laps. They hated it at the beach club when she swam laps. At the beach club they thought of the pool as a vast bowl of moisturizer that she slipped into whenever they got just a bit too hot. Serious swimming was considered an aggressive act. Serious swimming caused waves and waves of smeared makeup.

The afternoon traffic had thinned out along the coast. The lunchers were all napping, Cindy thought, and the businessmen hadn't left their offices. *I could end up doing this for the rest of my life,* Cindy thought, despite her good mood. *I could spend the rest of my life driving from restaurant to club to house. What a depressing thought.* But she had known she had to stay down here this year and help Daisy. Daisy was too proud to ask for help, but Cindy had seen the small signs of panic in her mother. Daisy was used to swimming through every room as though she absolutely knew that people would part as she approached, so she could make her own progress. Lately Cindy had seen her hesitate just before she went into rooms full of people, and if there was a mirror nearby, she often did a quick fast sideways glance which was absolutely against all of Daisy's rules. Daisy's number one rule had always been that if you did your best, dressed your finest before you left the house, then you never checked another thing because it was too late anyway.

That was part of Daisy's style, a well-thought-out carefreeness as though she just happened to look this way: perfect, without any work.

Not a woman in sight had ever believed that, of course, but Daisy didn't really worry an awful lot about what women thought, though this year she had tried to cultivate a few women friends, Marge Banning and Harriet Lowe, but watching Daisy try to talk to other women was like watching someone learn sign language. The words were the same as she normally used but somehow she was awkward and uncomfortable around women. She'd thought of them for so long as her competition that to try to think of them as friends practically required a vaccination. Her tongue froze in the act of giving a confidence to women, whereas it could spit right out the most outrageous flattery to men.

At the club Cindy changed quickly, marched right out onto the deck and mounted the low board. From the silence that dropped over the pool you would have thought she was perched on a cliff above Acapulco Bay. No one except the blond guard who was watching her with his mouth open ever got on the board, and he only did it to skim the pool.

Cindy raised her arms in fair warning of what she was about to do, watched that the water was clear and dove in smoothly but not so smoothly that when she surfaced half way down the pool she couldn't hear the rumble of disapproval.

She swam her hundred laps back and forth, head down, evenly until the lane was cleared for her, and then she got out, and picking up her towel, marched back toward the cabanas. The pool attendant slipped her a wink as she went by, and Cindy winked back. She felt a whole lot better. The butterflies in her stomach were gone. She dressed quickly and saw that it was now nearly five thirty. If the traffic was heavy, she thought, she might even be late, so she threw on her clothes in a rush and hurried out of the club.

The traffic was sitting absolutely as still as death on the coast road. From the way the traffic looked they might have been trying to evacuate the city, cars moving forward inch by inch. Now she was sure she was going to be late, and she kept craning awkwardly forward to see what was holding everything up.

The clock read six thirty as she rushed through the front hall and up the stairs two at a time.

"Dinner, Miss Cindy?" the housekeeper called after her.

"I'll have a sandwich," Cindy called back. She was taking off her clothes as she went down the hall. In her room she threw them in a heap, gathered up the skirt and blouse she'd left out and started to dress again.

There was a knock on the door. He'd called. She knew it before she even answered. Her throat was dry and her heart seemed to just drop way inside her. He couldn't come. She knew it.

She was still holding the blouse in her hand. She sat down on the edge of her bed.

There was another knock on the door. She hadn't realized that she hadn't answered the first knock. Her mind seemed to be reeling and she had a feeling of nausea. "Yes?" she said weakly.

The door opened slightly. The housekeeper poked

her head around the corner of the door. Cindy felt tears coming to her eyes, and she was glad the room was still shadowed from when she'd tried to take a nap.

She waited for the news.

"Miss Cindy?" the housekeeper said kindly, "you don't want dinner? You don't feel well."

The relief that flooded through Cindy made her light-headed. "I feel wonderful, Julia," she said leaping off the bed and starting to put on her blouse.

"But no dinner?" the old housekeeper asked. "A sandwich?"

"I have a date," Cindy giggled, pulling her head through the opening of the blouse.

"Ahhh!" Julia said smiling. "A date." All was clear. "What time?"

"Eight o'clock," Cindy said contemplating her reflection in the mirror. She looked okay, she thought.

Julia checked her watch. "Eight o'clock," she cried out, "you'll be late!" She hurried off to get Cindy a sandwich.

Cindy contemplated her reflection in the mirror. She looked okay, she thought again with satisfaction. Not Daisy perhaps, but okay.

3

Raul was leaning against a palm tree in the parking lot of the shopping mall. Behind him the marquee of the movie theater shone unnaturally bright in the twilight. He had his arms crossed over a plain white tennis shirt that showed off his body to its best and was wearing jeans and tennis shoes.

Cindy pulled the silver Mercedes into the nearest spot. Raul came over slowly and for the first time she noticed the way he walked, almost bowlegged, rolling and very deliberate as though he wouldn't be hurried for anyone. She liked that right off.

Most people noticed the car, even her own friends, and said something about it, but he ignored it. "You look great," he said as she got out.

"I was almost late," she apologized. "I got stuck in traffic coming back from the beach club." She had just said the words when she regretted them. Raul wouldn't have ever been to the beach club, she didn't think, and if he did, it would have been to work.

If Raul was embarrassed by that, he ignored that as he had ignored the expensive car. He smiled, a wide, white smile and put his arm very naturally about Cindy's shoulders as they walked up toward the theater. Cindy had been fumbled at by lots of boys from her own set, a lot of the time when they had a drink or two out in the back of a dance, and she had always just sort of seized up, but Raul's arm just felt good. More than that it felt right.

She knew a lot of boys and considered them friends but that was because she'd known them most of her life and their parents too. This was different already, she knew that.

Raul paid for their tickets and they went in. The people waiting to see the next show were cordoned off while the theater was cleaned of popcorn canisters and Coke cups. Cindy noticed other girls looking at Raul and she felt a kind of pride that she was with him. "What did you do today?" she asked.

He shrugged, but that smile played around his lips. "Worked." He had dropped his arm now and was just standing tall and natural beside her. He feels at home in the world, were the thoughts that went through Cindy's mind. The boys she knew, there was a good reason for saying that their parents owned the world and they would, too, but she didn't think any of them had ever looked quite as comfortable as Raul did. He looked as though he knew a good deal about the way the world worked, and it wouldn't get him down, no matter what.

Cindy tried to identify the feeling that she had standing beside him in the garish theater lobby. It took a moment before she had to sort through smug and proud and excited, but she finally got it: she felt safe with him. And she'd only known him for a few days and not spent any time at all with him really, except for lunch. She looked at him, with his arms crossed lightly over his chest again, so the muscles of his biceps swelled, standing there looking over the crowd casually and she thought, *He's physical! That's why!* The boys she knew were usually athletic and many of them were as well built as Raul, but it was more like something they had studied: tennis or sailing or horseback riding. Raul looked as though he fitted right into his body and was used to it and knew how to use it.

She wished suddenly that Jenny could be here to see her. Then just as quickly she was glad she was alone here with Raul. All her life she'd wanted to share everything that happened to her with Jenny who was her best friend, but this was hers alone, and she wanted it that way.

She felt somehow that she was different too. That didn't make any sense. But she didn't want to be the old Cindy everyone knew, who made crazy lists and cracked jokes all the time. She wanted to be someone different for Raul, someone she had been saving inside herself for a long time. And having old friends around wouldn't let her do that.

The usher dropped the rope and the crowd filed into the theater. Any other time Cindy had been on dates, the boys had tried to make conversation all the time, asking her questions that they probably already knew the answer to. And she'd asked the same sort of questions back, like where they went to school and what they would do when they got out of college. Raul just smiled at her like they'd known each other a while. They walked on into the dim theater, side by side.

"Halfway?" he asked her, gesturing to the row smack in the middle of the theater.

Cindy nodded, and he led her along the aisle to the two seats in the middle. He slipped into the seat which was too small for him and slid forward so that his knees were almost eye level. Other people filed into the theater until it was half full and the lights went out. Cindy got nervous all of a sudden, wondering if he would make a move here. She'd liked that arm on her shoulder when they were walking up to the theater, but she wasn't prepared for a struggle if that had been the preliminary to something more.

But the credits ran and the movie began, and Raul knitted his fingers under his chin and watched the movie through the V his knees made on the back of the seat in front. Cindy got absorbed in the story which was a mindless tale of men chasing men in cars. She turned once to find Raul watching her in the dark, his black eyes glittering. He didn't smile or behave as though he had been caught doing something he should apologize for. It was Cindy who smiled finally, then she found herself doing something she would have bet money she wouldn't have done: she reached out and put her hand over his where it now lay on the arm of his seat. The top of his hand felt warm and dry, suntanned if that could be possible, and Cindy felt a reaction like she'd never felt before at the touch of someone else, excitement and fear all mixed together, but happiness too. Raul rolled his hand over gently and took hers in his, then they turned back to the movie on the screen and that was the way they watched the end of the picture, hand in hand.

When the lights went up they kept on sitting where they were until the theater was almost empty. Raul got up finally, still holding onto Cindy's hand and they went out into the Miami night where stars could be seen high in a blue-black sky and a jet was planing in over the city toward the Fort Lauderdale airport. "You want something to eat?" Raul asked her quietly.

She didn't. "Okay," she said.

Raul seemed at a loss for a moment. Cindy wondered if he was worrying about money and a small panic hit her. She didn't know how to say it, but she wanted to tell him that she didn't want money to enter into this. She would eat carrot sticks with him on the beach happily if that was what he could afford.

But what he said was, looking to the left and right in the sky. "Up the coast or down the coast?"

Cindy shrugged. "Doesn't matter," she said. Then she added, "Your town."

He looked quickly at her when she said that, but he didn't reply. She reached into her purse and handed him the car keys as though to confirm what she'd said. He knew the territory; she didn't. She flew into Palm Beach every year with Daisy, had done so year after year, but until Daisy had given her this car, she couldn't have found her way to the beach club alone. Cindy lived in a very tight little circle: home, the club, the houses of friends and some selected shops.

I might as well have lived on an island off the coast, she thought as Raul looked at the keys to the Mercedes in the palm of his hand, for all I know of the coast.

"I don't know," Raul said uncertainly, looking at the keys.

"You drove it at the spa," Cindy said.

"That was different," he said, looking at her. Most of the other cars in the lot had driven off. The mall was dark except for the theater. They were nearly alone with the silver Mercedes gleaming in the warm night.

"I'd like it better," Cindy said and to her horror, she could hear echoes of Daisy's own voice in her own. She'd learned something about flirtation from Daisy, no matter how much she'd resisted it.

"No women's lib?" Raul said smiling.

"Not about driving," Cindy said. "I've only had my license four months."

"I'll drive," Raul said at last.

He held the door for her and then got in carefully behind the wheel. The way he sat there looking at the controls, Cindy knew he was seeing it differently from when he just had to park it at the Spa. He fitted the key very slowly into the lock and turned on the ignition smoothly. He backed the car out and drove carefully out into the traffic. He didn't speak while he piloted the car through the city roads toward the freeway and soon they were flying along the dark freeway at an even distance from all the other cars heading south. Cindy shook her head and let the air take her hair. It would look like an egg beater hit it when they got where they were going, but she didn't care.

She saw Raul's hand reach out and she noticed how smooth his skin was, the way the fine black hairs lay along his strong arm and yet how delicate his fingers were as they turned the knob of the radio. He chose a soft rock station, kept the volume low and exchanged a smile with her as they flew on into the night.

They drove for nearly an hour before he turned off. The long drive had chilled Cindy, but she didn't want to say anything. She was glad though when he touched the signal and the little red arrow started to signal that he was about to take them off the freeway. All of a sudden, the noise of civilization came at them in a rush as the wind was left above on the freeway and the car slid down into the sparse traffic of one of the smaller beach towns. The sound of the radio was lost to car engines and louder music. The stars were dimmed by neon signs above small beach front restaurants.

"Kind of honky tonk," Raul said. "But I like it. The Gold Coast. Anything's possible here."

And they would meet no one either of them knew out here, Cindy thought gladly.

He drove them into the center of town. It seemed to be a small strip of three blocks of nightlife along the water's edge. As he parked the car, a girl on roller skates, dressed in tight shorts and a halter top, wearing a Walkman, skated past. She took one good long look at Raul, at the car and then at Cindy, then did a double take.

Kind of hard to believe, huh? Cindy thought. A boy who looked like Raul, with the money for a car like this and he's out with a turkey like me. Her spirits took a small dive, but Raul had come around and reached out to help her out of the car and the feel of his hand, warm and dry, reassured her. She forgot about the girl who had spun off into the night, hips swinging in rhythm to the sounds only she could hear.

Raul looked up and down the beachfront, and he got a chagrined look on his face as though he hadn't seen it before. "Guess I could have chosen better," he said looking sheepish.

Cindy put her arm through his. "I like it," she said. And she did. She felt she was in some foreign place a lot more than an hour's drive from Palm Beach.

Raul put his hand over hers, as they walked out onto the boardwalk. "I think Florida must have looked like this twenty years ago," he said. "That's why I like it."

Cindy didn't understand but she didn't say anything.

They walked along for a while. Stands open to the beach sold hamburgers and tacos, meat on skewers, Cokes. One or two people were drinking beer out on the sand, out of the direct glare of the streetlights. The beach was a long strip to their left, an even dark barrier between them and the silver plain of the ocean that stretched away to the horizon where a tiny ship was pasted against a black backdrop.

"People must have come down here from all over," Raul said, picking up his explanation eventually. "Sort of like a gold rush, you know. You still see it, people coming here to get away from wherever they came from, driving down with trailers hooked up to the back of their cars. First winter they sort of beam all the time at not having to shovel snow. Can't get over it. Couple of winters later, they're natives grumbling at all the new people coming in." He laughed. "Strange, huh? Everyone wants a barrier put up across the state borders when they've gotten in. Before that, they think everyone has a right to come south. Once they get here, they don't want any more people. Guess that's life," he said. "Pull up the ladder, Jack. I'm safe."

His voice was soft, not bitter. Cindy wondered how old he was. She'd thought he was about her own age, sixteen, maybe seventeen, when she met him the other day. Now she wasn't so sure. He sounded older, as though he'd seen a lot more than any of the boys she knew. The boys she knew thought of themselves as very sophisticated. They'd traveled a lot and knew how to behave in expensive restaurants, how to get themselves to Europe if they had to, and what to do when they missed a connection, but Cindy could see that you could stay right where you were and maybe learn more important things about life.

"How old are you?" she asked suddenly.

He cocked his head at her. He smiled, "Seventeen," he said.

She'd been right the first time. Still, there was something more . . . she searched for the word she wanted and got it . . . more settled about him than the boys she was used to. He didn't seem to want to run off and eat up all of life the way they did, like kids set free at a party. The boys she knew had had everything they ever wanted for the most part, and you'd think that would satisfy them but when they got out of school they went sort of crazy, many of them. Look at Ronnie Webster rushing up and down the coast high as an eagle, picking up drunk driving tickets.

"You?" he asked.

"Sixteen."

He stared at her for a while as though he couldn't

really take her word for it. She knew she had always looked older than her age. But what he said was, "You're different," which was what she had been thinking about him, but it shocked her to have it said aloud back.

She laughed. She'd known all her life she was somewhat different. She'd never quite fitted any mold, and that had made her feel left out a lot of the time. For a while she'd thought it was having Daisy for a mother, and she'd blamed her for it. Daisy was full of surprises, and for a couple of years there, Cindy had come close to hating her for it. You never knew what you were coming home to with Daisy. Life for Daisy was one large stage set, a play with herself at the center. Jenny had always understood because Jenny, though she lived a more or less quiet life with Cassie out at Land's End, didn't have a regular set of parents like everyone else either. "That's true," she said.

Raul didn't look as though he was about to rush off, now that he'd discovered her secret. Cindy had a running dialogue inside, a dialogue she'd learned to keep to herself except when Jenny was around. It was like a tape playing what she was seeing and when she let others in it, they usually looked at her as though she was only steps away from the ward they'd hauled off poor Susan Lockwood after her break-down, so Cindy had learned to keep it quiet.

"You should be glad," Raul said, as though he was reading her thoughts. "It's easy to be like everyone else."

The night had taken a strange turn, and Cindy wasn't sure she quite followed what had happened or if she liked it. This was getting close to serious business. She'd looked forward to a date, not analysis.

Still she couldn't help what she heard herself say. "That's not true, you know," she said, which didn't help lighten up the mood. He stared at her as though he hadn't heard. She wasn't sure she had heard right herself but she knew it was exactly what she thought, so she figured she must have said it aloud. It was her own voice that had said the words, and she meant them. She could have kicked herself for letting the tape go on high volume and letting the words out. She'd probably spoiled her chance for a romantic date on the Florida coast with a boy who looked like a movie idol from silent pictures.

But she'd gone this far, so she might as well finish what she'd started. "It's tough to be different," she said.

"It's tough being *anybody*," he told her.

That took her breath away for a minute. She'd expected sympathy or at least a few lines of discussion about how it was neat to be different but a burden. She found she was laughing. "Okay," she conceded, "it's tough to be anybody."

The mood lifted right away and they were back in the tropic night. She liked the way he'd been able to do that and she realized that she didn't know anything about him at all. Up till now, she'd thought that she was onto a really great date with a terrific looking boy. Now she thought she better take a long look at him. There were still waters there, as Cassie would say. "What about you?" she asked.

He didn't need her to spell it out. "Oh, I'm going to be the richest man in Florida some day," he said quietly.

That made her want to laugh too, but she kept it in, in case he thought she was laughing at him.

But he was too wise for her. "You think I'm kidding, don't you?" he said, putting his hand over hers where it lay on his arm to reassure her that he wasn't getting back into those gloomy waters they'd navigated a few minutes ago.

"Why should I?" she asked. "Almost everyone I know spends their time trying to get richer. Even my mother." This was the first time they'd talked about money, but it was out now, right there for them to look at the whole problem, and here too, it didn't seem charged with problems. It was just there. The problem seemed to have been mostly in Cindy's head.

"But I'm going to be different than most of the people you know," he told her, but it wasn't an insult. "I'm going to be real content."

He would too, she thought. She knew it. "How are you going to get all this money?" she asked him.

"Work for it, I guess," he said. "Seems to me that money just sort of flows all about, doesn't it, and you just have to make a little dam and catch some of it for yourself." He looked about the beach with the stands that they had left behind, with their lights in the air and the people on the boardwalk. "Still lots of opportunity around, seems to me. I'd like to have a lot of businesses, but first I want a health spa of my own. People are never going to stop looking after their own hides so that should make money, then I'd like to go on to other things, movie theaters maybe, because people like to be entertained and restaurants because they want to eat. Making money seems to me sort of a nice simple thing to do, once you set your mind to it. Knowing what to do once you get it, that seems to be the problem from what I see down here."

She believed him. She didn't know why she did, but she did. Yes, she didn't know why, she thought, looking at him standing there a few inches from her in the Florida night, his shirt whiter than any white she'd ever seen in the shadow and his tan darker because of it. She believed him, because he had the same assurance as the old men she had met around the clubs and private houses all her life, not the sons and the grandsons who inherited the fortunes, but the old men who had made them. The old men sat off to the sides and their eyes took in the big houses and the lawns and the clothes and the jewels, and you could tell what they were thinking, but keeping their thoughts to themselves. At gatherings they drifted together as though only they understood each other.

"How are you going to solve the problem?" she asked.

He had an answer to that too. He'd given all this a

lot of thought. "I'm going to figure out what I really like doing, and that's the only thing I'm going to do," he said. "I like a nice house and I like to scuba dive, so a boat would be nice. I like to eat, but I don't care if I have the biggest house or the biggest boat or fancy food, so I'm not going to worry at all about what other people think, just figure out each time what *I* think and what *I* want and I'm going to do that. All the people I see are rushing about worrying about what everyone else is doing, they don't seem to be having much fun themselves."

"Why do you have to be the richest, then?" Cindy asked.

"Why not?" he said. And he laughed. "You got to have a goal."

She knew it was coming before he had moved a fraction of an inch and her blood started up in a rush of its own, pulsing through her body, but when he reached out and gently put his hands on her arms, she thought her heart would hammer its way out of her chest. It was pounding so hard, he pulled her gently toward him, and her body sort of molded against his as he turned his head slightly above hers and fitted his mouth over hers and then she seemed to get lost in a new country for a while. Time lost its meaning, and when she came back to the present, it was as though she were a different person. It took her a few seconds to realize that they were still standing there on that tacky boardwalk and the beach was there and the stands and the far-off people.

She caught her breath. She was very happy, but she was frightened too. "You're a menace," she said with some of her old spirit rising to help her out of this moment.

He was looking at her with those black, black eyes. "I told you I figure out what *I* want, and I go out and get it."

Cindy was calmer. She was also hungry, and still a little scared. "Well, what I want," she said, "is something to eat."

She had expected some disagreement. If this was as smooth a seduction as she thought it was, he would have some block to that request. But what he said was, "Okay."

He dropped his arm lightly about her shoulder again and they started back toward the lights.

Cindy was relieved, but she was sort of offended, too, that he hadn't put up more of a fight. He *was* a menace, she thought. She'd have to be on her guard.

4

Daisy's muffled voice came through the telephone. "Darling? Are you there?"

"Yes, Mother, I'm here." Cindy was half asleep. The word was out before she could stop herself. She heard the silence on the line, a humming that might very well have been anger. Daisy was adamant that she not call her *Mother.* "Daisy?" Cindy said louder.

"I tried calling you last night," Daisy said. "The cook said you'd gone out."

"I went to a movie," Cindy said. The white lie came out as smoothly as *Mother.* If she'd said she'd gone on a date, Daisy would have wanted all sorts of details, his name for one, and Cindy wanted to keep that to herself. She didn't want to share one second of last night with anyone else.

Daisy must have had a lot on her mind, Cindy

161

thought, for all her seeming air of frivolity, since she didn't usually miss much. But she let that go by. "I'm going to be here a few more days," Daisy said. "Will you be all right?"

"I'm fine, Daisy," Cindy said, stretching luxuriously in bed. She was aware of every inch of her body as she never had been before. The light through the pale green sheer drapes made the room as mysterious as the underwater of a pool, and Cindy imagined herself floating along pushed by mysterious currents. "How are you?" She didn't want to come right out and ask the question, Are you going to have your face lifted? No one had actually thrown that on the table yet, though both of them knew what Cindy was talking about.

There was another silence on the line. "I'm all right," Daisy said finally, but it was unlike Daisy not to know exactly how she was. Daisy kept her thumb figuratively on her own emotional pulse pretty closely. She'd been her own greatest hobby all her life.

"Sure?" Cindy asked.

Another pause. "I just can't make up my mind," Daisy said, and again both of them knew what she was referring to.

That was unlike Daisy, too, not to be decisive. Daisy usually could make quick decisions when it came to the point. She had five marriages and five divorces behind her to attest to that.

Cindy wondered whether she should push any further into the question. Daisy had never discussed that type of thing with Cindy. Daisy, for all her self-involvement, had behaved more or less like a stern mother toward Cindy. She'd draped Cindy around behind her it was true, but she also exercised that same decisiveness on Cindy's behalf: always made sure that Cindy was well taken care of, knew that she was loved, though in Daisy's own weird way, and did what Daisy considered normal things for a school girl. But they'd never had much in the way of girl-to-girl talks. Cindy had long ago accepted that Daisy wasn't capable of girl-to-girl talks. She'd been an only child and adored by adults herself. Then she'd been the most beautiful debutante in Savannah, and then lately she'd just been Daisy, which had been quite enough. She didn't know much about sharing. She just sort of assumed that people were happy to take a full interest in Daisy. But she'd done her best as a mother, given that she was stuck with the person she was and, Cindy thought, unaware that other people weren't exactly the same.

Cindy asked, "How's New York?"

Daisy brightened up. "Wonderful," she said. "Everyone's got out their furs."

Cindy asked, dreading the answer, "Would you like me to come up there to be with you?"

She could tell that Daisy was touched. But Daisy's answer was typical of her way of dealing with emotional offers. "I don't think so, darling. Christmas isn't that far off and we have to be back there for the Samuels's dance. It would be a waste for you to fly up and down this late." Daisy was nothing if not practical.

Neither of them said anything for a few seconds. Daisy became aware of the cost of the empty long distance line. "Call me if you need to," she said. Then as though she wanted Cindy to know that however much Daisy hated needless waste, none of those rules applied to Cindy. "And if you want to come up here, just call and you can be on the next flight."

"No!" Cindy said too fast. Then, covering, "The weather is really great. No clouds."

Even after all these years and all the calls, neither of them knew how to say good-bye comfortably, so Daisy did what she usually did when she was uncertain. She got brisk. "Good-bye, then."

"Good-bye . . ." She almost said *Mother* again. But she managed just in time to say, "Daisy," before the line went dead.

Cindy replaced the receiver on its hook. She lay where she was savoring the quiet. She wondered what time it was and stretched to peer at the clock: eleven o'clock! She'd always woken at seven no matter where she was. Always. She had been conditioned by years of boarding school bells.

She felt guilty for no reason at all and almost got out of bed, but she just rolled over, hugged her pillow and let herself float off into a dream of last night, of Raul, the drive down the coast, the food and conversation they'd shared. He made her laugh. He was arrogant and conceited but she liked that. He was sure of himself, confident. The evening had passed in what seemed like a second, and driving up the coast, they saw dawn cracking the horizon with a band of gold.

Cindy had wanted to drive him home, but he'd told her that she could let him off at a bus stop in Miami and he'd be fine. It would be easier for her to get back on the freeway heading for Palm Beach, he told her, and she didn't push it. When he got out of the car, he'd leaned over and just lightly brushed his lips against hers. The kiss she'd expected all night came finally and just as unexpectedly as the whole evening, with wonderful timing, for it thrilled her and left her driving home alone, singing along with the early morning disk jockey.

Raul, she knew, had had to work today, so she got up finally filled with a real guilt at her own sloth, took a long shower and dressed in shorts and a blouse. She went downstairs in her bare feet and found that a place was set in the dining room for lunch.

The cook heard her come into the dining room and came out. "Could I have a salad?" Cindy asked.

The cook, who was well-rounded herself, disapproved of salad, calling it *rabbit food,* but she agreed, knowing that that was what Daisy would have wanted too, if she had been home.

A maid came in while Cindy sat humming to herself, looking out at the garden. There were no butterflies this morning that she could see, but if they'd stayed up as late as she had, they were probably safely tucked into the sleeves of the honeysuckle vines, bright wings folded safely in sleep.

The maid said, "There was a call for you earlier." She handed over a slip of paper. "A young man," she added.

Cindy wanted to leap up shrieking, "Why didn't you wake me?" But her years of training kept her in her seat, though her heart had sort of turned to ice and the day had somehow lost half its light.

The maid said, "He told me not to wake you." She was still holding out the piece of paper. "But he made sure I wrote down the message and repeated it to him."

Cindy took the folded sheet of paper. The maid was looking at her strangely. She unfolded it with dread. The message said, "Same time, same place."

When she looked up, the young maid was trying to stifle a giggle. Both of them let go. They giggled at the message until the cook came back in and shooed the maid out.

The cook put down the plate of salad, bright fresh leaves of green and strips of carrot, olives and avocados, a mound of salad enough to feed a family of rabbits.

Cindy doused it with dressing, then began her lunch, thoughtfully chewing. She held onto the little slip of paper all through lunch until she went to put it safely in her drawer upstairs.

5

Raul said, "None of that seems real to me. I was born right here in Florida." He gestured with a lunge backwards toward Miami. "Right here in *Miami*. I don't remember any of the days with big houses and servants. Sometimes I even think my grandmother makes it up."

Cindy watched the way the sunlight fell on his face. He was telling her about his background. His family came from South America. His father had fled their country before Raul was born and brought his own mother and two young brothers to the United States. She wondered if he had Indian blood somewhere in his background. He looked almost Inca sometimes, very proud, with his head held tall on the broad column of his neck, but then he would smile and the flash of white teeth would take away all the mystery and he'd be a boy again.

Cindy knew a lot of people from other countries and many of them from South America. Most of them, however, had taken fortunes with them when they left. They lived in huge houses up and down the coast, in lavish cooperative apartments in New York or in mansions in Bel-Air.

"My father," Raul was saying, "was made into a bitter man by losing all his money. He'd been a lawyer in Colombia, but when he came up here, the only work he could get was as a messenger at first." Raul sighed. "I just got tired when I was a kid listening to stories about the past, the past, the past . . . I wanted to talk about what was on television, or baseball."

Cindy reached out and put her hand on his bare knee. They were alone on a beach that Raul liked, a beach not far from the city but which required holding back a fence to gain access to a dusty road. All the land here belonged to the government. After starting to develop it, the government had then dropped the project, so it looked like a war area, broad jungle roads, bulldozers left abandoned, trees fallen over. But when they bounced their way through that in the Mercedes, suddenly there was a broad stretch of yellow sand and the ocean bright blue to the horizon without a boat in sight. A tall stand of palm trees arched toward the water providing some shade. Here Cindy had set out the light lunch she'd brought them on a pure white tablecloth.

It was Saturday. Raul had the day off. But they'd gone out together every night for the last three days. Somehow he had become her best friend in that short time, almost closer than Jenny.

She had no past with Raul. She was just Cindy as she revealed herself to him. And he had had no past, no real past, until today. "Things happen to you," Raul was saying about his father. "And you just have to go on. You can't let the past trap you."

His leg was thickly muscled and smooth. His tan was darker than any he'd ever seen. "You're not going to college then?" she asked.

He shook his head impatiently. "No," he said, "I could have, I think. I didn't make much effort. I think it's a waste of time for me. Maybe it's good for some people, but I think for what I want, it's just putting off what I have to do."

"Become the richest man in Florida," Cindy teased him. "You might need every second you have for that," she said. "Lots of competition."

"You must have thought I was a class-A jerk when I said that."

"No," Cindy admitted laughing. "I believed you. It was me I was worried about when I saw I believed you."

"Well, I might, you know," he said, taking hold of her behind the neck and looking directly into her eyes from the distance of an inch. When he touched her, Cindy's blood still started pounding like it had a marathon to run. "That would show you."

He leaned forward then and kissed her. If she

hadn't been lying full out on the sand, she would have fallen dead at his feet she was sure. The kiss went on very slowly for a long time. When he took his lips from hers, they felt as though they'd been rubbed smooth by a soft cloth. She was breathless.

Cindy took a deep breath and blew it out. This was deep water. She'd watched Daisy through a few romances, and she'd known how Jenny had been struck by lightning and left burning last summer by Thorn. She wasn't sure she was ready for it.

Still it was nice to find that love was as powerful as it was, frightening as that might be. It was like finding Santa existed after all.

She rolled over on her back. The sun felt hot on her skin, and when she opened her eyes, she was blinded for a moment. Her sight came back slowly. A jet stream streaked the sky white. She looked at Raul. "You want to go for a swim?" she asked.

He got to his feet. From where she was lying, his legs seemed to stretch up to where the plane had left the white trail, long and brown. His hips in his black suit were broad and strong, and his chest was muscled with the definition that came from hard work, not a gym. He reached down, took her by the hand and pulled her slowly to her feet.

She thought he might be about to kiss her again, so she ran off down the beach and plunged into the water, throwing herself in fully as soon as it was safe. The water felt icy on her hot skin and she breast-stroked out underwater.

When she came up, she saw the dark form of

Raul's body as he swam toward the horizon with steady, strong strokes. Cindy treaded water watching him swim farther and farther out and she found that she was afraid for him. He seemed a long way off. Just as she was about to call out, he turned and started back. When he reached her, he was hardly breathing heavily, though she was out of breath from treading water.

"I've got to go in," she said. "My legs are tired."

He dove under her, sweeping her legs into his arms, and when he came up, he was holding her against his chest. His face was shiny with water, and his hair slicked back smooth against his head. Cindy leaned forward and kissed him carefully and held the kiss, laughing inside herself until she felt him sinking underwater. She jumped free as he gasped for breath and swam toward shore.

She was sitting, shaking the water out of her ears, when he strode up out of the water. His legs truly were bowed slightly, she noticed. She liked that. It made him different somehow, unique. The water pushed away from his thighs in small waves.

"So," he said, "you would drown me with love, would you?"

She laughed at him. "You want something to eat?" she asked, looking at the lunch.

"Is there anything left?"

She reached into the hamper and brought out some fruit. "Grapes," she said, and going back in again, "and a peach."

He took the peach. Cindy lay on her side watching

him as he sunk his teeth into the flesh of the peach. Then he put grapes into her mouth one by one. The juice ran down the side of her mouth.

"You could be an actor," Cindy said.

He smiled at her happily. "You think so?" he asked.

"Sure," Cindy said teasingly. "You're vain enough."

He had lifted her before she even knew he was about to move and taken her, squealing, back down to the water. He dumped her in the shallows and walked back alone to the beach towels.

"Macho man," Cindy said angrily as she shook the sand out of her ears when she got back.

He was lying on his back with his eyes shut, taking in the last of the afternoon sun. He didn't say a word.

"You *could* be an actor," Cindy said again reluctantly. "Have you ever thought of that?"

He shrugged. "No," he said.

"I've seen plenty of them," Cindy said. "My Dad produces pictures out in California."

Raul opened one eye. "No kidding," he said.

Cindy made a sour face. "It's not as big a deal as it sounds. Producing pictures is sort of like running a small grocery store if you really know what's going on. Not much magic."

"How would I get to be an actor?" he asked.

The sun was coming down the dome of the sky slowly. The sunset colors had already begun, peach and green stripes smeared across the sky. "There's a couple of ways," Cindy said. "You can work at it or you can just sort of stand still and let it hit you. There are other ways, too, but those are the main ways. One takes talent, the other takes bone structure."

"You don't know that I have any talent," he said.

"Fishing," she said.

He smiled and rolled onto his side. "It'd be sort of neat to be an actor," he said. "Have a big television series every week, women throwing themselves at me, houses, cars."

"I thought you weren't going to be rich like the rest of us," Cindy said.

If she hadn't known him, she would have thought he was blushing. "Rich is rich sometimes," he said, and looked away up the beach to where a big ocean-going yacht was coming in, planing up two white waves at its bow.

"You don't have to worry about the women," Cindy said. "I'm pretty sure they'll throw themselves at you anyway."

The words gave her a strange feeling as she said them. She was cold suddenly. The late afternoon had lost none of its heat, but she shivered. She knew why too. She had seen Daisy with her men. Some of them worshipped Daisy, and she walked all over them, but there had been a couple where Daisy nearly lost control. That hadn't been nice to watch. They'd walked over Daisy for a while, till she got a grip and bounced them. Daisy knew what was what, and at a certain point, she took action to protect herself.

And then there had been Thorn with Jenny last summer. Thorn, in his own way, was a pretty neat guy and Jenny was the best, but in the end that had been a train wreck too. Thorn had lost twenty pounds when Cindy had seen him last, and from the last sight she saw of Jenny from the train as she left that terrible day in the summer when Thorn had been unmasked, Cindy thought Jenny was about to come apart.

Raul saw her shiver. He stood up and took the beach towel from under him and shook it free of sand. He put it around her shoulders. She shivered again, but for another reason: she could smell his own masculine smell on it. Like orange peel that had dried in the sun.

Other sounds came to them now on this isolated beach. A squawk of a parrot in the trees behind them, voices that seemed to be nearby, then died down. Cindy was aware of Raul as she had never been of any other boy. She could sense him moving about, putting the things into the luncheon hamper. She knew he was aware of her too. A lot of the good feelings of the day seemed somehow to be in jeopardy, but something else was in the air.

Cindy didn't move at all. She just sat there letting Raul gather everything up. He took his time.

When he came down the beach to her, he was still only wearing the black suit, though the evening was upon the whole coast. Stars were already visible, pale in a translucent gray sky. A crescent new moon hung across the far city.

When he touched her shoulder, she looked up and rose without a word. The towel dropped from about her shoulders. He leaned to pick it up, but she put her hand on his arm. Half bent over, he looked up at her, black eyes gleaming, and rose slowly. He kept his eyes on her, locked with hers, as he put his arms about her and then his face seemed to move closer and closer, almost floating in the warm air as his lips touched hers.

Cindy closed her eyes.

Abruptly, he stepped back. When she opened her eyes he looked angry. He wasn't looking at her. He was leaning over again to pick up the towel. "We should get out of here," he said roughly.

Cindy felt the blood rushing up her whole body. She wanted to die right there on the spot. He thought she had thrown herself at him. He was contemptuous of her. He was already walking back to where the hamper was. She watched him pull on his clothes, his jeans, the tennis shirt in anger, without looking at her.

She had to follow him because her clothes were there. She could have left him there, she realized, because it was her car off under the palm trees. But she wouldn't.

Tears stung her eyes as she put on her shorts and the oversized white man's shirt she'd been wearing earlier. They went together through the trees to the car. He didn't offer her her car keys back, but when he started the car, he took his frustration out on it, pushing the key in too fast and then grinding the gears. They shot out over the rough dirt roads like they were in a race.

He drove fast and carelessly, never looking at her. They came to the freeway and the traffic heading back to the city. He wove in and out of the cars. The other cars had their lights on. He forgot to put on the Mercedes's lights. Cindy reached over and flicked the switch. He looked at her then, once, fast, and she thought she saw something other than anger and contempt there. She thought she saw anguish, but she couldn't be sure. She wanted to speak to him, but she had made enough of a fool of herself for one day. She took a deep breath and looked away, out across Biscayne Bay. She closed her eyes and opened them again. She had been right before she thought. Love was a downer, a risk. She should have stayed with the jokes and the long lists of crazy thoughts, that there were only two thousand people in the world, or why were all lifeguards blond. Real life was too unexpected, too raw.

The car bounced off the causeway, and he piloted it through the traffic to where they always met in the same parking lot near the theater. He lived nearby, she figured, though she had never asked, and he'd never taken her to his home. The parking lot was empty, too early for the theater, too late for the mall shoppers.

He left the engine running when he got out. Cindy

slid over with difficulty. He closed the door on her. She looked at her hands on the wheel, waiting for him to say something. She wouldn't look at him.

"Good-bye," was what he said.

The words stung her. She swallowed. But anger saved her too. She put the car roughly in gear and shot past him heading for the entrance to the lot.

The tears held off until she was safely away, speeding home to Palm Beach.

6

Four days passed. Cindy was floating in a world of shadows and light. She lay in her bedroom staring at the ceiling. The pain would go away at some point. She knew that. She had watched Daisy. She wished Daisy was here so she could talk to her. And at the same time she was glad that no one was here. If she got through this she would never have to go through it again. Everyone said first love was the best and the worst. Well, true to form, Cindy was going through it all in one gasp.

The housekeeper came to her room and knocked on the door, asking if she was okay.

"I'm fine," Cindy told her. "I just want to sleep."

But she knew that if she didn't get up and eat something, they'd call Daisy. Daisy always left secret instructions that Cindy knew nothing about, *mother's* instructions, Cindy thought of them, feeling safe and warm for them all the same—that the staff watch Cindy and get in touch with her if anything went wrong.

So Cindy got up and trudged down to the dining room and ate soup and salad. Then she went back up to her rooms and threw it all up again.

She made herself take a hot bath and that helped. She fell back into bed and slept another ten hours and when she awoke it was to a room that was awash with a strange light. She got out of bed feeling some strength again and she opened the drapes to find that there had been a storm while she slept. Hurricane season was October, so it wasn't a hurricane, but this had been strong enough, she thought. The garden was littered with dead palm fronds and the bushes stripped of flowers that lay plastered against the walk, sodden, slowly dying. But the sun was coming out through a clearing sky, making shadows along the walks and you knew, just looking, that soon the garden would bloom again, the palm fronds would be cleared away and all signs of the storm lost.

She looked thinner, she thought, when she looked in the mirror. Daisy would be proud of her. Daisy hadn't called, she realized. Not in four days. Something was up. Maybe she was already in the hospital having her eyes done.

Cindy was ravenous. She showered, dressed in slacks and a clean pink blouse and went down to breakfast. The cook peeked in at her as she ate her way through juice, toast, cereal and eggs. The word was spreading through the house that she was fine.

But after breakfast she lost some of her confidence. The day stretched before her empty. She didn't want to go to the beach club and she couldn't go to the spa. She went back up to her room and tidied up her own personal things, moving about her famous notebooks in their drawer, her jewelry, her scarves. She took out the notebooks and read through them. They seemed to have been written by a stranger. She could hardly recognize her own hand in the words.

She ate lunch and went into the sunroom to think. Life, with a capital L, stretched away from her like a sentence. She knew why Daisy spent so much time flitting from one appointment to another like the fate of Western Europe was in her hands. This wasn't enough. Not for Cindy anyway. When Daisy got back, they would have to talk. She had to go to college. She thought about what she might study. Anthropology struck her as interesting, the study of cultures, of people. Who knows, maybe one of her crazy theories would prove correct. Maybe she would win the Nobel Prize for proving that there *were* only two thousand people in the world.

She played with the idea of the Nobel Prize for a while. She liked the sound of that.

Then something happened toward late afternoon. When she thought of it later, she thought it might be Daisy's blood coming out in her. Daisy was a fighter for all her southern charm. Her father was tough and nice, but when it came down to the line, Daisy had more guts.

Cindy made the decision. She went upstairs and got her purse and her car keys. She almost lost courage there for a moment. Then she took a deep breath, looked at herself in the mirror, and left the house before she could change her mind.

She hit the rush hour traffic but she was in the theater parking lot before she lost her courage. When she got there she drove slowly along the rows of cars as they thinned out, not sure of what she expected, not sure really why she had come. But she knew she had to know something, something important.

He lived nearby. She knew that. It wasn't until she had given up and her spirit was draining away with the color of the evening sky that she realized it would have been easier, more sensible, to have waited until tomorrow and gone to the spa. But she didn't want to see him there, at the spa. It was too much like one of the rich, hysterical women who had their hearts broken with an embarrassing predictability each year by tennis pros or fortune hunters.

The marquee over the theater was dark. Then she saw that there was no show tonight. No sign of a picture. No title.

She turned off the ignition and sat there alone in the car. It was stupid to have come. Well, at least she hadn't made a scene. Another scene, she corrected herself.

Maybe she was the one who should be the actress. She liked drama well enough, she thought wryly.

The lot was almost empty, the cars all about had moved away. She wasn't sure at first that it was him. He was standing near the theater, leaning there. But she recognized the pose and the white tennis shirt from the spa.

She just sat there waiting. His arms were crossed across his chest. Finally, he dropped them and came to her, walking slowly, the bowlegs taking their time bringing him to her.

When he was standing near the car, she found that she was very angry. She looked at him, waiting for him to say a word so she could explode. She had made a fool of herself, but he had been part of it. He had set her up. But he wouldn't look at her. He crossed his arms again and stood there near the fender, looking away.

"Would *sorry* help," he said finally, and his words were as soft as the air.

No, she thought. "You want to take a drive?" she asked. She felt as though she had been beaten up. The words were the words of two people who had known each other a long time, gone through a lot, not the words of two teenagers who had just met a week ago.

He nodded. She went to slide over, but he said, "You drive. It's your car."

She didn't protest. It *was* her car. He got in and she drove out down the freeway, knowing right away where they should go. He seemed to know too, and he let her take them there, reaching out only once to put on some soft music, soft rock, the way he had the first time they had gone down the coast. She found her way there as though she had known exactly where she was going. As she slowed to pass onto the coast road he looked at her and she looked back, a look that had forgiveness in it, understanding, and something more.

The evening people weren't out in force yet. When the engine died, they sat side by side looking at his strip of beach and beach stands.

"Why?" she asked finally. She had to at some point.

He didn't want to answer. Finally he said, "I knew who you were all along. Your mother's kind of famous in her own way. I knew she was one of the richest women down here. So you—"

That made sense, more sense than she liked to admit. "So it was all a play. I was just another rich girl to be taken for a ride."

"Not all of it," he said. Then he looked at her and smiled. *"You* picked me up," he reminded her.

She made a face at that.

"But I couldn't do it," he said.

She was afraid to ask the next question. But she did. "Why?"

He drew a deep breath. "Because I like you. I didn't want to use you."

Nothing very much happened to change the evening right then, but it was as though a huge weight had been lifted off Cindy. She found she was smiling.

He snuck a glance at her. He was afraid to ask his own question, she knew, and she let him suffer a bit. Then he said, "Truce?"

She considered. "All right," she said finally.

Then both of them wanted to get on with life. He said, "I've been wearing these clothes all day. I want to go home to change. You want to have dinner tonight?"

"You bet your life I do," Cindy said starting the engine again.

He turned the music louder and the trip back up the coast went by faster than it had before either going up or going down, and except for looking at each other a few times and smiling, neither of them seemed to need to say anything.

When she got off the freeway he gave her directions to where he lived. His parents' house was a plain, clean bungalow in a back street. Children were playing up and down the street. They looked at the car and at Raul and he shrugged. "You know what everyone's gonna think," he said.

"Who cares what everyone thinks," Cindy said, "if we know what we think."

"Okay," he said. "As long as you're warned."

"Oh, I've been warned," Cindy said.

But before he got out, he leaned over and they

kissed once again, a nice, familiar kiss, that held a lot of promise.

"Can you find your way back here?" he asked as he stood by the car.

"Are you kidding?" Cindy said.

He laughed and she drove off.

7

Daisy was waiting in the sunroom when Cindy went in. "You're back!" Cindy exclaimed.

"I got worried," Daisy said. She was lounging on the rattan chaise by the window. The blinds were open and she was looking out at the garden. Nothing had been done yet to her face at any rate. The tiny lines were still there. Cindy was so glad to see Daisy she ran over and dropped onto the chaise by Daisy's knees. "You sounded strange on the telephone," Daisy said. "Are you all right?"

"I'm fine," Cindy said. Then she added, "Now," and squeezed Daisy's hand. "You shouldn't have rushed back."

Daisy looked hard at her daughter. She made up her mind that Cindy was all right. "Well," she said, "I can't decide about the surgery anyway." She looked out at the garden again, and then back at Cindy. "Marge Banning had it and they pulled her so tight she looks as though someone is firing a gun behind her ear all the time."

Both Cindy and her mother giggled. "Well, I think your . . ."—Cindy was careful to search for the right words—". . . your very little lines look . . ."

"Look what?" Daisy asked suspiciously.

"Look sort of distinguished," Cindy teased.

Daisy shot straight upright. "Distinguished!" she protested, but even she had to laugh. "Well," she said, dropping back against the cushion. "I earned them anyway. They're all mine, every last wrinkle of them. Nobody gave them to me."

She thought about that for a few moments while Cindy thought how nice it was to have Daisy back. Then Daisy said, "Shall we celebrate my old age by going out to dinner?"

Cindy looked down at her hands. "I can't," she said. Then she looked at Daisy. "I have a date."

Daisy's face sort of changed for a second, then her well-known control took over. "A date," she said brightly. "That's nice, honey." Her pleasure for Cindy was real, Cindy could tell. "I'll get to meet him, then, anyway."

"No," Cindy admitted. "Not tonight anyway." Daisy was looking at her warily. "He doesn't have a car," Cindy rushed on. "I have to pick him up."

Daisy said nothing for a few moments, and then she said, "Well, perhaps he'll come to the house for dinner one night soon, and I can meet him then."

Cindy wanted to hug Daisy. "He'll like that," she said.

"Good, then," Daisy said. "That's settled." She got up off the chaise. "I think I'll have a hot tub and a tray in bed. What time will you be home?"

"Early," Cindy said.

"Come along to my room and tell me all about it," Daisy said. She kissed Cindy on the cheek. "Now go off and get ready."

They went out together into the hall. Daisy turned toward the kitchen to give orders for her dinner. "Oh, what's his name?" she asked.

Cindy was halfway up the stairs. "Raul," she said.

Daisy didn't blink. Cindy gave her high ratings for that and loved her for it. "Ask Raul for dinner next Thursday," Daisy said, and went on through to the kitchen.

Cindy went on up the steps one at a time: she was filled with a happiness she couldn't ever remember feeling.

If you've enjoyed this book...
...try four exciting First Love from Silhouette romances for 15 days—free!

These are the books that all your friends are reading and talking about, the most popular teen novels being published today. They're about things that matter most to you, with stories that mirror your innermost thoughts and feelings, and characters so real they seem like friends.

And now, we'd like to send you four exciting books to look over for 15 days—absolutely free—as your introduction to the First Love from Silhouette Book Club.℠ If you enjoy the books as much as we believe you will, keep them and pay the invoice enclosed with your trial shipment. Or return them at no charge.

As a member of the Club, you will get First Love from Silhouette books regularly—*delivered right to your home.* Four new books every month for only $1.95 each. You'll always be among the first to get them, and you'll never miss a title. There are never any delivery charges and you're under no obligation to buy anything at any time. Plus, as a special bonus, you'll receive a *free* subscription to the First Love from Silhouette Book Club newsletter!

So don't wait. To receive your four books, fill out and mail the coupon below *today!*

First Love from Silhouette is a service mark and registered trademark of Simon & Schuster, Inc.

First Love from Silhouette

THERE'S NOTHING QUITE AS SPECIAL AS A FIRST LOVE.

$1.95

First Love from Silhouette

70 ☐ MORE THAN FRIENDS Stuart	80 ☐ ENDLESS SUMMER Bayner	90 ☐ SURF'S UP FOR LANEY Caldwell
71 ☐ THAT CERTAIN BOY Malek	81 ☐ THE MOCKINGBIRD Stuart	91 ☐ R_x FOR LOVE Graham
72 ☐ LOVE AND HONORS Ryan	82 ☐ KISS ME, KIT Francis	92 ☐ JUST THE RIGHT AGE Chatterton
73 ☐ SHORT STOP FOR ROMANCE Harper	83 ☐ WHERE THE BOYS ARE Malek	93 ☐ SOUTH OF THE BORDER Kingsbury
74 ☐ A PASSING GAME Sommers	84 ☐ SUNNY SIDE UP Grimes	94 ☐ LEAD ON LOVE Hart
75 ☐ UNDER THE MISTLETOE Mathews	85 ☐ IN THE LONG RUN Alexander	95 ☐ HEAVENS TO BITSY Harrell
76 ☐ SEND IN THE CLOWNS Youngblood	86 ☐ THE BOY NEXT DOOR Youngblood	96 ☐ RESEARCH FOR ROMANCE Phillips
77 ☐ FREE AS A BIRD Wunsch	87 ☐ ENTER, LAUGHING Leroe	97 ☐ LAND'S END Stuart
78 ☐ BITTERSWEET SIXTEEN Bush	88 ☐ A CHANGE OF HEART McKenna	98 ☐ ONE OF THE GUYS Makris
79 ☐ LARGER THAN LIFE Cole	89 ☐ BUNNY HUG Harper	99 ☐ WRITTEN IN THE STARS Marshall
		100 ☐ HEAD IN THE CLOUDS Lewis

FIRST LOVE, Department FL/4
1230 Avenue of the Americas
New York, NY 10020

Please send me the books I have checked above. I am enclosing
$_____ (please add 75¢ to cover postage and handling. NYS and
NYC residents please add appropriate sales tax). Send check
or money order—no cash or C.O.D.'s please. Allow six weeks for
delivery.

NAME _____

ADDRESS _____

CITY _____ STATE/ZIP _____